THE INVISIBLE EMPIRE

John L. Jenkins   Mark W. Weaver

RECONCILIATION PRESS, an imprint of
Trinity Rivers Publishing, Manassas, Virginia

The Invisible Empire

www.reconciliation.com

Copyright © 1997 by John L. Jenkins and Mark W. Weaver

Published by Reconciliation Press, an imprint of Trinity Rivers Publishing, Manassas, Virginia 20108-0209.

All Rights Reserved. Written permission must be obtained from the publisher before any portion of this book may be legally duplicated in any form, except as allowed by the Copyright Act of 1976 (Title 17, U.S. Code). Such permission is not required when quoting brief portions of this book within critical essays, articles or reviews, if standard bibliographic credits pertaining to this book are therein displayed.

With the exception of recognized historical figures, organizations and places, the characters and organizations described in this novel are fictional; any resemblance to actual persons, living or dead, or actual organizations or places is purely coincidental.

Front and back cover drawings: Steven Phillip Morales.

Cover design: Laurel Vaughan.

Educational Consultant: Horace G. Danner, Ph.D.

Printing and binding: United Graphics, Mattoon, Illinois.

Library of Congress Catalog Card Number: 97-80635

ISBN 1-888565-03-9

Authors' Note

We often compare our nation's founding to a two-fold cord of good and evil. Some colonists came to escape religious persecution and to establish a nation governed by godly laws. Others came in search of gold and a quest for wealth where fierce individualism would make its own laws.

Unfortunately for millions of America's and Africa's indigenous peoples, their freedoms were stolen for the benefit of others. Our founders' original belief that "all men are created equal" quickly gave way to generations of bloodshed, broken treaties, and slavery. Our great ideals of freedom did not prevent great wounds of injustice that have yet to be healed some two hundred years later.

The failure of our ideals can make the study of history painful and difficult for Christians. In history's mirror, we can see our own reflection in the lives of others. We also often discover that there are no convenient villains. It's much easier to point an accusing finger at someone else.

However, historical fiction can help us see more clearly by putting us into the shoes of characters who traveled our history's darker byways, characters who struggled and overcame the century-long spiritual conflicts that have shaped our nation and our culture.

That is why we wrote *The Invisible Empire*, the first book in the Century War Chronicles Freedom Series, and a companion and chronological predecessor, *Beneath the Sky of an Angry God*, the first book in our Discovery Series. These two, seven-book series follow the lives and interconnected adventures of young people through critical points in 19th and 20th century America.

What has been will be again, what has been done will be done again; there is nothing new under the sun.

Is there anything of which one can say, "Look! This is something new"? It was here already, long ago; it was here before our time.
(Eccl. 1:9-10 NIV)

Freedom means different things to different people. For some, freedom is so much a part of their lives they never have to think about it. For others, where they live, what the color of their skin happens to be, and when they were born, freedom may seem more like hope than reality.

The Invisible Empire is an exciting story that gives both young people and adults fresh insight into the challenges and dangers faced by young blacks in mid-19th century America as they sought to experience that most crucial ideal called *freedom*.

I hope the next time you find yourself talking to someone about freedom, you'll think about this book and the important reminders it offers readers of every generation.

    Dr. Chalmers Archer, Jr.
    Author, *Growing Up Black in Rural Mississippi*

1

The Liberty Bell presided silently over Independence Square from its vantage point atop the State House tower. On this Tuesday afternoon in April of 1872, a late spring breeze brushed over the two-thousand-pound bell's surface.

Twenty-six years had passed since the last time the bell rang out as it celebrated George Washington's birthday back in 1846. The weathered and cracked bell had loudly tolled over much of America's history, including a call to the first public reading of the Declaration of Independence in 1776. The bell's inscription could still be read: *Proclaim Liberty Throughout All the Land unto All the Inhabitants Thereof. Leviticus xxv.x.*

Below the bell, sixteen-year old Josiah Washington stood with his back to the old red brick State House. He faced a semicircle of four older boys pressing in like a tightening noose.

The tallest of the four boys stepped forward, a lock of brown hair curled down between his menacing eyes. He pressed his lips into a determined line and moved his fists in small, deliberate circles like a boxer.

"No more cat and mouse! See how you like this!"

His right fist shot straight at Josiah's mahogany, oval face.

Josiah jerked his head to the right but his opponent's knuckles caught him above his left eye. He retreated several paces across the lush grass. Blood trickled from the corner of his eye and joined the blood already flowing from his nose.

He watched through angry eyes as his opponent raised his fists and moved in for another swing. Josiah wanted to raise his own fists, but he knew that would only make his troubles worse.

Out of the corner of his eye, he caught a glimpse of long strawberry blond hair. He glanced to the left and grimaced—the girl who had caused this trouble was back again!

"Stop it, Adam!" The slender girl stepped between them. "I tripped. Josiah was just trying to keep me from falling!"

Josiah sucked in his breath, his eyes darting back and forth between the girl and his opponent. How'd she know his name?

The boy called Adam hesitated, then shook his head from side to side. "Doesn't matter why, Christine. He grabbed your arm. I saw him do it. No colored's going to get away with touching you when I'm around. He's gonna pay!"

Christine grabbed Adam by the arm and pleaded. "No! If you care about me at all, stop! Stop right now!"

"I said he's gonna pay!" Adam edged her aside and balled his hands back into fists.

With a gasp of frustration and with her eyebrows scrunched in worry, Christine gathered her skirts. She turned and ran across the lawn, back toward the busy noonday street.

Adam's eyes followed Christine for a moment; then, with a sigh, he brandished his bloodied knuckles and eyed his three friends. "All right! Let's finish teaching him a lesson. Next time he'll think twice before grabbing the likes of Christine Thompson."

Adam's friends laughed and spread out to Josiah's right and left.

Backing toward the base of an old maple tree, Josiah felt the brush of leaves on his neck. He realized that he had two choices: try to defend himself or—

Josiah gambled on the second choice and spun around. His eyes searched the old maple and found what he was hoping for—a low-hanging limb. Fear pumped through his legs. He grasped the limb and swung his feet up.

His mind screamed. Scramble! Scramble for your life!

Hot in pursuit, Adam mistimed his jump and crashed solidly into the tree. He cursed and shook his fist. "You wily skunk, you! We'll get you yet! Let's see how well you dodge rocks, standing up there on a limb."

Doubt rippled across Josiah's dark face as he looked up.

Plenty of branches were within reach. But what good would climbing higher do him if he got thumped with a rock and fell? He was still dizzy from Adam's punch and the first rock thrown when he had been trapped behind the State House.

Suddenly Adam's cocky smile withered into a frown.

The square-shouldered manager of the nearby Freedom Press hurried up the cobbled walk beside the State House, a scowl forming on his nut-brown face. Her arms folded stiffly in front of her, Christine stood by the corner of the building and scowled.

With a sharp nod of his head, Adam signaled his friends. "Seventh and Walnut!"

Relief washed over Josiah as he watched the four young men scatter in opposite directions. He quickly climbed down the tree and found himself face to face with Toby Sykes, his boss and only real friend, the manager of the Freedom Press' weekly newspaper, the *Freedman's Journal*.

Toby ran his big hands over his close-cropped, salt-and-pepper hair and sighed. His dark eyes flashed with frustration. His high cheekbones and angular face, usually home for a broad and relaxed smile, were now hardened with concern.

He examined the shallow gash over Josiah's right eye. "Let's get back to the shop and clean that cut. Might need stitches."

They started across the back lawn of the State House toward Chestnut Street. Toby reached into his back pocket and offered Josiah a handkerchief.

As he wiped his blood on the handkerchief, Josiah looked around for the girl who had caused all the trouble. She was nowhere to be seen.

Would Toby blame him for what happened?

Toby raised his hand. "No need to explain, son. Miss Thompson's already told me the whole story. There's no excuse for what Adam Vestry and his friends did to you. None."

Josiah stuffed the handkerchief into his back pocket and frowned. Christine Thompson—the Reverend's daughter. Now he remembered. He'd seen her at the Methodist church where he and Toby attended Sunday services.

Pausing at the corner, Josiah and Toby waited for a long wagon train loaded with bulging sacks of grain to ramble by. Streetcars and omnibuses shuttled Philadelphians of both colors back and forth across town. Commerce was booming, and people hungered to read about it.

As they crossed the street, Josiah looked up at the Public Ledger Building, six stories tall and nearly a block wide. The building, home to Philadelphia's biggest newspaper, the *Public Ledger*, stood directly across the street from the State House and the Liberty Bell.

Around the corner and two shops down was the Freedom Press. The narrow, brick two-story building was squeezed between an insurance agency on one side and a wheelwright shop on the other.

Walking down the sidewalk, Josiah noticed how straight and tall Toby held himself. Toby never let anyone steal his dignity.

Josiah shook his head. Dignity.

He thought back to his first day on the job as a printer's devil two weeks ago. He recalled how Toby leaned back in a chair, put his hands behind his head, and stared thoughtfully into the air.

"Ten years," Toby had said, his voice swelling with pride. "Ten years."

"What about 'ten years'?" Josiah remembered asking him.

Toby had stared him down with a look of amazement. "Why, son, I know you have a proper knowledge of history. I'm talking about ten years of freedom!"

Now, as they walked up to the door of the Freedom Press, Josiah stiffened, just like he had when Toby first spoke those words two weeks earlier. Lincoln's Emancipation Proclamation, issued ten years ago in 1862, may have legally freed the slaves, but it had also cost Josiah's parents their lives.

With the taste of blood again on his lips, Josiah lowered his head and followed Toby inside. For all the freedom that emancipation and the Civil War had given him, he didn't feel very free.

2

Josiah clenched his teeth as Toby cleaned the wound. The ointment stung fiercely. Tiny white stars floated before his eyes. Josiah gripped the edge of the stool and fought back the anger burning on his tongue.

Toby nodded, inspecting Josiah's eye. "God's watching over you. You'll heal fine without stitches. Unclench those teeth and smile."

The print shop manager sat back on his stool. He placed the bloodstained cloth in a pan of water on the nearby layout table and dried his hands on a towel.

Toby took a deep breath and shook his head. "So, you've got Adam Vestry and his gang after you? It's a tough world, isn't it? Learning when to stand up for your rights and when to back down is not an easy lesson for any man."

Josiah did not answer. He stared across the Freedom Press and its open twenty-by-thirty foot work area, beyond the printing presses to the backward letters painted on the storefront window. He silently spelled the word to himself: F-R-E-E-D-O-M.

But what was freedom, really? Choosing what you did with your life? Having the right to vote? Owning property? Though Toby managed the Freedom Press print shop and its weekly paper, the *Freedman's Journal*, the owner, Sam MacDonald, was white.

Toby sighed. "Adam's father is a very influential man. He manages the *Public Ledger's* national desk and reports on important issues that affect the whole country. He's a sly one, too, pretending to side with freedmen—but after that riot near the docks, his true colors are starting to show."

Worry tinged Toby's voice. "The Freedom Press doesn't need any more enemies than it already has. With Sam in Washington for the week, you and I have got to defend the shop and its reputation."

An omnibus rolled slowly by the shop window, the driver clucking his two-horse team.

Josiah studied the people inside the bus. Three freedmen sat crowded in the back row while the middle and front rows of seats were only sparsely occupied by whites. Resentment edged into Josiah's thoughts. Was that freedom—riding all jam-packed in the back of a bus when it was less than half full? Where was the freedom in that?

Rising from his stool, Toby put his hands on his hips. "Are you listening to what I'm saying?"

Without moving his head, Josiah raised his eyes to meet Toby's. He gripped the edge of his stool. Anger roiled inside of him as his eyes locked squarely onto Toby's.

Toby grabbed his stool and planted it with a loud thump in front of Josiah. He sat down heavily, resting his elbows on his lanky knees.

Josiah refused to drop his eyes. His lips tightened into a line.

Toby's eyes flashed. "Young bucks like you think that nobody else understands! Like you're the only one who knows how it hurts to be owned by somebody else. I know how it feels to be split up from your family on an auction block and never know if your name came from your parents or from your owner!

"So, you get punched and cut in a fight and start sulkin' because you think you've got it rough! I've seen dozens of young men like you whipped 'til their backs turned red. I've seen a man shot dead because he tried to learn to read on his own."

Shifting his weight on the stool, Toby leaned forward. "I know it's hard to accept, but have you forgotten that white men also spilled their blood to make us freedmen? I lost a dozen good friends in that war, and only two of them were freedmen. In fact, the best friend I've ever had is white. Sam McDonald and I have worked together since '65. And don't you remember that before the war Sam's wife was murdered because he was an abolitionist and stood up for men like you and me? He paid a steep price for freedom, too."

Josiah lowered his eyes. Toby's words stung worse than the ointment in the corner of his eye. He knew Toby was right. Thousands and thousands of whites had fought and died in a war to defeat the Confederates and to end slavery.

But Josiah's memories and his anger were too strong. He jumped up from the stool and crossed the room to the front window, keeping his back to Toby.

Toby pushed himself from his seat, then stopped halfway across the room. His countenance hardened just like it had behind the State House when he had driven the ruffians away.

"Don't turn your back on me, young man. After your parents died, Jedediah McClintock took you into his home and treated you like a son."

The emotions that had been building up inside of Josiah exploded from his mouth.

"The McClintocks weren't my parents! My parents were murdered, and it was whites who killed them!"

Toby shook his head slowly from side to side. "Anger and bitterness like that's gonna eat you up. Jed and his wife gave you clothes, a good home and an education. They made sure you learned to read and write! And they gave you the respect that's due any man. Tell me that's not true!"

"I'll tell you what's true," Josiah said sourly. "Half an hour ago, I kept a girl from falling on her face in the street and got beat up for it. And two minutes ago, while we were sitting right here, a bus goes by—freedmen crowded in the back, whites in the front! That's what's true and don't say it's not. You saw it yourself."

"Let it go, son," Toby rejoined, his voice softening. "It's going to take more than ten years to undo hundreds of years of hurt. You've got to find something good to give your life to. If you let resentment win out, it'll eat at your insides 'til you have nothing left to give."

Suddenly the steam went out of Josiah, and the sadness returned. "Either we're freedmen right now or we're not freedmen. Something's got to be done."

He looked up at Toby. "Something."

"That's why Sam McDonald and I opened The Freedom Press and started our weekly newspaper, the *Freedman's Journal*," Toby explained patiently. "We want to help rebuild this country, to change the way people think, to help them forgive.

"Sam cared enough to give you this job. Now that your stepparents have moved to Boston, you need to make the most of this opportunity."

Josiah nodded weakly. His heart ached and his forehead throbbed.

Toby sighed. "Take a short break. Let your head clear while I clean the printing presses and set the type for this afternoon's run of the church bulletins. I'll call you when I'm ready."

Josiah nodded. Avoiding Toby's eyes, he walked between the presses to the back hall and climbed the stairs to their living quarters on the second floor.

He proceeded through the kitchen and past the two middle rooms where Toby and Sam slept. His room, at the end of the hall, had the best view with a window overlooking Chestnut Street.

Plopping onto his bed, Josiah closed his eyes. He couldn't deny the good things Toby had said about his stepparents, Jedediah and Anna. Jedediah deserved his promotion and the job in Boston, but Josiah really missed them. He remembered how before they left for Boston they had bought him a denim shirt and a pair of shoes. Anna had cried when they hugged goodbye. Deep down, he did appreciate all the kindness they'd shown him—ever since the first day they took him in nearly ten years ago.

Ten years. The ghastly image of his real father's tortured face overwhelmed him.

He squeezed his eyes shut to hold back the memories from that tragic late summer night in 1862. However, like a spark in dry leaves erupting into flames, painful memories burst into his mind, as hot and bright as the night they happened.

3

In September of 1862, Josiah and his parents escaped from slavery through northern Georgia, the Carolinas, Virginia and Maryland. Their trek took a little over two weeks. They traveled by night and hid by day. In the darkness of some unknown benefactor's root cellar or basement, fear faded and sleep came.

Josiah remembered lying on his back with his small bundle of ragged clothes under his head, his mother's warm body on one side and his father's on the other. How much they slept during their trip he wasn't sure. Only one thing he knew: they were freedmen.

President Lincoln's proclamation had spread through the South like wind blowing fire over a field of dry grass. And when the Underground Railroad came through northern Georgia one rainy September night, Elijah and Colette Washington and their six-year-old son bought one-way tickets north to freedom.

Excited and fearful, Josiah and his parents had bounced over the rutted road in the back of a tarpaulin-covered wagon and crossed the Mason-Dixon line. Josiah smiled, recalling how his mother's rich voice broke forth into sweet praises and thanks to God Almighty for His saving power.

Once over the Mason-Dixon, their speed northward picked up considerably. Less than twenty-four hours later, they arrived hungry and weak at a Methodist church on the south side of Philadelphia.

Philadelphia! Heaven on earth! A place where thousands of blacks, some former slaves just like themselves, lived free!

That night they'd stayed with a farmer and his wife who lived close to the church. Josiah and his parents slept in the barn—a barn that was nicer and drier than their shanty in Georgia had ever been.

In his mind's eye, Josiah could see the thick oak beams above the hayloft in the farmer's barn just as they had looked ten years ago.

His parents lay beside him again, one on each side and both sound asleep for the first time in weeks. He could still remember the clean, almost-sweet smell of soap. They'd each taken a long, hot, steamy bath.

The smell of the dry hay returned, and then the other smell, too, the horrible smell that had haunted his dreams for ten years: the acrid smell of smoke.

He remembered pushing himself into a sitting position in the hay-covered loft. He remembered being groggy and confused—then, suddenly, he heard a horse whinny. He recalled rubbing his eyes and wobbling to his feet near his sleeping parents.

Shadows bobbed about on the barn wall opposite the loft. He stumbled to the hay door at the end of the loft, unlatched it and swung it open. He stood in the darkness and looked at the barnyard below dimly lit by the moon.

Three men sat silently on horses, rifles across their laps. Their hats cast shadows over their faces. Their leather saddles creaked. Moonlight glinted off the rifles' long barrels.

Bounty hunters! Josiah keenly recalled the fear that drove the stupor from his head, how he turned to wake his parents only to see a thick column of flame leap up from the middle of the floor and illumine the entire loft in amber light.

He screamed and shook his father by the shoulders again and again and again. His mother remained motionless despite the noise and jostling.

By the time he roused his father, the flames had spread up the far wall, licking wildly along the oak beams up to the ceiling. Dazed but now aware that the barn was on fire, his father lurched to his feet. He grabbed Josiah and dragged him toward the open moonlit square at the end of the loft as the flames leapt into the hay behind them.

"Daddy! Daddy!" Josiah remembered crying.

The fire's deafening roar drowned his father's reply.

Josiah's memories sharpened and slowed. As if it were just yesterday, he could feel his father's arms wrap tightly around his chest and pick him up from the loft floor. Seconds later, he felt the terrifying sensation of his legs dangling out the hay door and banging against the outside wall of the barn.

He had clutched frantically at his father's outstretched arms as he glanced at the horsemen below. The man in the middle raised his rifle and fired twice.

His father screamed. Josiah twisted and strained to look up as his father's grip loosened.

The next moment was frozen forever in his mind.

Smoke swirled around his father's head; a spreading red bloom of blood covered his right shoulder. Tears streamed down his cheeks. His eyes were filled with sadness and loss that stabbed Josiah to the center of his soul.

Before Josiah could cry out, a burst of red heat engulfed them. His father tore his arms and hands free from Josiah's chest and determined grip. A halo of fire circled his father's face and Josiah fell away.

For a split second, a starry sky and full moon filled his vision.

Then, for a moment, all went cold and black.

Josiah blinked away a blurry film of tears and cut short the memory of what happened next. Pushing himself into a sitting position on the bed, he stared at the narrow desk and oil lamp wedged in the corner near one end of his bed.

On the desk stood an inkwell and an old pen. Beside the pen lay a new, blank journal for keeping a diary. Toby and Sam had given it to him as a gift.

"Commit yourself to keeping an account," Toby had explained

with Sam looking on. "There're things in life worth remembering, good and bad. Sam always says, 'If you forget the lessons God teaches you in times of trouble, you'll have to learn them all over again.' "

Toby's words echoed back to Josiah. He wiped his eyes and looked up at the ceiling. No! He wasn't going to write down his thoughts and feelings. He wanted to forget what happened that horrible summer night in '62. The barn. The fire. The man with the long-barreled pistol who had shot his father in the shoulder and then—.

Josiah lifted his head. The sound of a happy female voice below his window snapped his attention to the street below. Wiping his eyes, he leapt off the bed. The lump in his throat was almost gone.

Jerking back the curtains, he looked down into the street, shoving his pain back inside him.

"Angelina!" Josiah called out after clearing his throat and smiling.

After stepping away from her buggy, a young woman wearing a calico dress and a flower-trimmed bonnet turned and looked up. Seeing Josiah, she smiled broadly and waved.

Angelina was a beauty all right, with her smooth, light-almond skin, her warm, dark eyes and brown hair that hung to her waist when she let her braid down. Other than himself, only Sam and Toby knew that she had once been a slave and that Sam had adopted her as a young girl, not long after the Battle of Gettysburg. Fortunately, the color of her skin did not give away her African heritage. Having mixed blood could make life even harder than just being black.

Josiah sighed. Freedom? Something had to change.

Something.

He broke away from the window and scampered downstairs, the scrape on his forehead and the old wound in his heart temporarily forgotten.

4

Angelina stood beside Toby and studied the handbill. Josiah looked on with an approving nod.

"Father will love them," she said cheerfully. "I'm going to the telegraph office right now and see if his message has come in. He's supposed to let me know how many I need to bring down tomorrow morning on the train to Washington."

Josiah didn't understand why so much fuss was being made over some handbills and a little book. He wanted to ask Angelina but decided it would not be appropriate.

"When do you leave?" Josiah asked instead.

"At a quarter past nine. Father's made plans to meet me at the railway terminal on the Mall in front of the Capitol."

Josiah studied Angelina's smile. Plain and simple, she adored Sam and everything he did. After being away at Oberlin College in Ohio for two years, she was back home to help Sam and Toby with the business. The only thing as strong as her love for Sam was her devotion to God and the Bible.

"Toby, would you mind if Josiah comes with me to the telegraph office?" Angelina asked.

The print shop manager planted his hands on his hips. His eyes darted back and forth between two smiling faces.

"I suppose I'll allow it. Just be back within the half-hour. We've an important run to finish up and I'll need his help."

"Agreed." Angelina turned and winked at Josiah. "I promise not to keep your printer's devil from his work too long."

Toby frowned, his stance suddenly rigid. He politely nodded, walked away, and began to fidget with the closest printing press.

Josiah looked from Toby to Angelina. What had she said that bothered him so much?

He followed Angelina out the door, climbed into the buggy, and sat down beside her.

"There are some things best not mentioned around Toby Sykes," Angelina offered, "and I just brought up one of them by accident. Some days the word 'devil' does not set well with him."

She snapped the reins lightly and the buggy lurched slowly into the street.

"But you were talking about my job as an apprentice for the print shop. You weren't talking at all about the Devil," Josiah replied.

Angelina carefully guided her filly around the corner onto Sixth Street.

"Well, that's a long story and it's really Toby's story to tell." Though her eyes were fixed on the street in front of her buggy, Josiah could tell her thoughts were elsewhere. Her voice sobered.

"You know, Josiah, there's a war going on all around us. Most people thought the war ended when Lee surrendered to Grant at Appomattox. But anyone who sees America like God sees America knows that our nation's troubles are far from over."

Angelina gently drew in the reins as they approached an intersection, then urged her filly sharply left onto Market Street.

She continued. "You can see evidence of this war everywhere. What's harder to see is how the lines are drawn and who's on whose side. The uniforms are no longer blue and gray, and the weapons aren't made of wood and metal. The weapons and the war are inside our hearts and minds, and each of us must decide which side we're going to be on—God's side, or the other side."

As he considered her words, Josiah raised his hand and touched the small scab over his eye.

An image formed: Adam grinning, rearing back his arm and flinging the stone. Then he remembered trying to keep Christine from falling off the curb into the busy street, noticing the contrast of his hand on her arm, black on white.

Were those the colors of the uniforms Angelina was talking

about? Josiah shuddered. And which side was God's side?

Angelina's large brown eyes briefly met his. He wondered if she knew what he was thinking. It didn't take long for him to find out.

"Bigotry and hatred are enemies of God and weapons of the Devil. However, Josiah, they're not his only weapons and our plight is not the only battle. I know it seems that way right now. Just remember that a cunning general knows how to use a strong frontal attack to disguise his full intentions. And that, I fear, is what the Devil's really up to. This battle is but the first of many battles in a war fought by enemies we can't see with just our natural eyes."

Josiah scratched the side of his head and peered at Angelina. This was a different side of the young woman whose company he had come to enjoy—weapons and battles and wars inside of us, enemies you couldn't see with your eyes! The Ku Klux Klan was the only "Invisible Empire" he had ever heard about. And its members weren't really invisible with their flaming crosses and ghostly shapes on thundering horses! Lord have mercy on your soul if you were unlucky enough to see them!

The telegraph office was just ahead on the right. As Angelina slowed the buggy, Josiah jumped down and guided the filly to the curb. Then he ran ahead to open the door to the office. Angelina climbed down and they entered the office together.

Josiah liked coming to the telegraph office. The sound of the operators frantically clicking their keys fascinated him. Letters, words and sentences sent through thin wires to points far away. How could this be done?

Angelina walked to the counter and gave her name. Josiah stood by a wooden rail that separated the rows of operators and their machines from the entranceway. How fast their fingers punched the keys!

The door opening behind him caused Josiah to swiftly turn his head. A tall, wide-shouldered man wearing an expensive pinstriped suit strode into the office, his black bowler in hand. His stark white hair, sour face and deep-set eyes gave him a fearsome demeanor, and his confident saunter and the slight lift of his chin made Josiah feel uncomfortable.

As the man passed by on his way to the counter, Josiah's hand gripped the rail. Outside on the sidewalk, Adam Vestry stood with his arms folded across his chest, his eyes watching Josiah from beneath the rim of his cap.

Josiah quickly turned and faced the counter.

Angelina, with her telegram in hand, faced Adam's father. She arched her left eyebrow sharply upward. "Mr. Vestry, I'm surprised to see you here. I would think a big newspaper like the *Public Ledger* would have its own telegraph office."

Waylan frowned. "Miss MacDonald, if it were your business to know our paper's business, I might offer a reply. But it's not. Shouldn't you be busy with your father's nasty little two-cent weekly?"

"Little, yes. Weekly, yes. Two-cent, yes. But nasty?" Angelina retorted. "Just because we countered your article on the Second Street riot last week does not make our *Freedman's Journal* nasty."

"Almost a riot," Waylan snapped back. "Your father continues to make a mountain out of a mole hill. There was no mob trying to keep the Liberty Engine Company from putting out that fire. The firemen simply arrived ten minutes too late to save the building."

Angelina frowned. "Come now, Mr. Vestry. It's all quite obvious. Everyone is saying so. Why would the freedmen who own the warehouse shoot the firemen fighting to save it? Something is underfoot, something to make the freedmen look like rabble-rousers and anarchists."

"Miss MacDonald. Such speculation only promotes hostility. The *Ledger's* stories are fair to both sides. I cheer all decent Negroes who respect the differences between our races."

Josiah glanced back at the window. Adam unfolded his arms. His eyes locked on Josiah's for a moment, then suddenly slid away to Angelina and his father.

Why? Josiah wanted to ask. Why do you hate me?

A loud thump behind him made Josiah spin around.

Waylan Vestry slapped his hand on the counter a second time. Angelina's face suddenly paled. Waylan's deep voice seemed deliberate.

"This city will not permit violence as a means of getting one's way. I urge your father to warn his freedman readers in no uncertain terms. I assure you, the *Ledger* will do all it can to promote heartfelt cooperation with next Tuesday's annual celebration of the Emancipation Proclamation."

Waylan snatched his telegram from the hand of the clerk behind the counter. "Put it on my bill."

In three long strides, he was out of the office. Adam remained tight-lipped and then followed his father across the street toward a lamp and lantern shop.

The color in Angelina's cheeks gradually returned as she read her telegram. But what started as a smile melted into a look of concern. She folded the telegram and handed it to Josiah.

"Let's get you back to Toby."

They exited the telegraph office and climbed into the buggy. Josiah opened the telegram. Sam asked for three things: 1500 handbills, fervent prayer, and a room be readied for an overnight stay by one of his associates, Daniel Sweetwater.

That name was vaguely familiar? Where had he heard the name before?

As Josiah lifted his eyes from the telegram, a crack of thunder clapped behind them. They both turned and looked up. Dark gray clouds moving in from the southwest now shrouded the city.

The breeze picked up, too. Angelina drew in the reins to stop for a man chasing a runaway hat into the street. Ladies standing nearby scurried along, pressing down skirts and hanging onto bonnets.

Angelina and Josiah's eyes met briefly. Her look confirmed Josiah's fear. More than one spring storm was brewing.

5

The storm struck briefly and furiously, then passed, leaving blue skies and puffs of white clouds. Meanwhile, Toby and Josiah completed the print run of 200 church bulletins on time and with very little waste. Josiah cleaned the tabletop press while Toby studied the results of Josiah's typesetting.

"The columns and margins are nicely justified, son. The layout has a balanced look from top to bottom. Reverend Thompson's going to be mighty pleased with this run when he returns day after tomorrow. You've proven to me that you've got a real knack for composing."

Josiah grinned and kept cleaning the press as Toby carried the stack of bulletins to the front counter. His grin faded as he the name suddenly connected.

Reverend Thompson! It was the Reverend's daughter, Christine, who'd gotten him into all the trouble with Adam Vestry. But even as he wanted to blame her, he knew better. She had jumped in and tried to break up the fight.

"Mind my words, Josiah. If you continue to add diligence and perseverance to your natural talent, it won't be long until Sam will make you a full apprentice. Then he'll start paying you cash for your labor, on top of room and board."

Toby leaned back from the counter and stared up at the ceiling. "One of Sam's favorite quotes comes from Ben Franklin, 'He that hath a trade, hath an estate.' A young man couldn't aspire to hold a more honest or respected job than that of a journeyman compositor."

As Toby finished speaking, a long, mule-driven freight car

stacked high with lumber rumbled noisily by. The name of the company painted on the side of the car read: HONEST ABE'S. The print shop manager shook his head disapprovingly. The driver, a grizzly-faced freedman with mahogany-colored skin like Josiah's, was pushing his mules much too fast this close to the center of the city.

About to make a comment, Toby was stopped by a frantic cry, followed by a loud crash and the prolonged skid and screech of wood and metal over cobblestones.

Josiah dropped his cleaning cloth and bolted toward the front door, with Toby close behind. They burst outside and sprinted down the rain-drenched sidewalk in the direction of the State House, joined by other shopkeepers and pedestrians hurrying to see what had happened.

The freight car had spun sideways and flipped over in the middle of the intersection. Two mules lay trapped underneath, braying balefully, their legs twisted and crushed. The other two mules stood in a shallow puddle, snorting and stomping and straining on their twisted lines.

Pallets of scattered lumber littered the street and spilled out onto the sidewalk in front of the Public Ledger Building on one side and Congress Hall and the State House on the other. The driver ran to the nearest corner, calling for a gun to put his wounded mules out of their misery.

A tall man with white hair and deep-set eyes stepped from the milling crowd of onlookers. Waylan Vestry smirked and extended his hand, offering the driver his shiny long-barreled Colt.

The driver wasted no time. Standing over first one mule and then the second, he swiftly fired two rounds into their rearing heads. The braying stopped as dark, maroon ribbons of blood spread slowly out into the street.

Groaning, the driver slumped to his knees on the wet street.

Waylan walked calmly to the driver and snatched the pistol from his shaking hand. He cleaned the butt vigorously with a handkerchief, then spun it on his finger and slid it into the holster in one fluid motion.

Surveying the wreckage, Toby rubbed the back of his neck.

"C'mon, son. The man's going to need some help. The worst of it's yet to come. This is the second time in one week that an Honest Abe's freight car has been involved in a fatal accident with its mules—and this one right in front of Vestry and the Ledger Building! There will be trouble. Mark my words."

Josiah looked up from the growing pools of blood. Waylan Vestry sauntered toward the street corner, his hand resting lightly on the butt of his Colt. A shiver traced its way down Josiah's neck and back.

Then he looked across the street to the State House. His troubled eyes rose to the Liberty Bell and the old crack that ran down its front side.

He wondered if freedom for freedmen, like the Liberty Bell, would ever get fixed.

6

Adam buttoned his cotton shirt and stared into the oval, wood-framed mirror above his bedroom dresser. He ruffled his hands through his light brown hair and pushed a long curl off his forehead. He tried to work the frown off his face and lift the doubt that shadowed his hazel eyes.

He briefly thought about his trip to the telegraph office, then his father's story at the dinner table. Talk about dead mules and pools of blood had stolen his appetite. But what bothered him even more and had stuck with him all day was his own behavior with Josiah in front of Christine.

Adam returned to his bed and plopped down on his back. He studied the lantern's dancing orange pattern on the ceiling above his bed. He wanted to rid his mind of the hateful, ugly glare he'd seen in his father's eyes as he complained about the wagoner who'd had to shoot his mules. It was the same hateful glare Waylan had flashed at Sam MacDonald's daughter, Angelina, at the telegraph office. Sometimes he could not understand the intensity of his father's animosity or the innocent events which aroused it.

And that's what troubled Adam the most about himself—it had been an innocent event that had triggered his outburst against Josiah.

The late evening breeze fluttered the curtain as a silver shaft of moonlight fell across his nightstand. His thoughts drifted to Christine Thompson.

Adam pictured her face in the play of light on the ceiling. Highlighted by rosy cheeks dusted lightly with freckles, and framed by her long, straight strawberry blond hair, Christine Thompson almost always offered him warm smiles. He remembered the first time they had met during his last year of school. Something about that girl had made him look her way every chance he got. Once he had gazed into those serious, blue eyes, he never wanted to look away. Now she was almost seventeen and even prettier!

Meeting Christine again complicated things. It had been so simple before when it was just the Walnut Street gang. Work a short day for the *Public Ledger*, then roam the streets of Philadelphia and stir up a little harmless trouble. Raise a ruckus. Have fun!

What would the gang think if he started seeing Christine?

Thoughts of Christine made Adam reach down and rub the scab on his elbow he had got as the result of chasing Josiah and crashing into the tree. After seeing Josiah grab her arm, well, he had just reacted.

Then his pride had kicked in. What had Christine expected him to do? Take back his words? Right in front of his friends?

Adam chuckled. Christine sure had a mind of her own, defending Josiah like she had! And she was right, he knew that. Though he and Christine had never talked alone for more than a few minutes together, Adam Vestry believed Christine Thompson would have been his girl if he had only asked her.

At one time, anyway.

Adam sighed and cradled his hands behind his head. Yes, the more he really thought about it, the worse he felt about what he had done. And it was more than just something with Christine. It was about his own anger and how easily it took control of him.

Over the past few years, something dark and ugly had worked its way deep inside his father. At first, Adam thought it had something to do with his mother's death a year ago. But he knew that his father's ugliness toward blacks had started long before she had wasted away with fever. Had his father always been that way? Or, Adam considered, maybe he had been too young and naive to notice his father's bigotry.

A frown returned to Adam's face. Though his father had never enlisted in the Army, he had served as a newspaper field reporter and covered a number of important campaigns and events, including Gettysburg, Lincoln's Emancipation Proclamation and Lee's surrender at Appomattox. The issue of slavery had been settled—except in the Deep South where some Southerners did not seem to accept that the war was actually over.

But this was Philadelphia. So then, what motivated his father now?

Adam flipped over onto his side, his thoughts drifting back to Christine's pleading face and flashing blue eyes as she stepped between him and the young black man she had defended.

Josiah turned up the lamp and pulled back the chair to his desk. He sat down, his eyes moving from the pen to the new journal.

He could hear Toby cleaning pots and pans in the kitchen. Outside his window, the commotion from the accident had finally died down. The hurried clip-clop of a solitary rider passing by interrupted the sporadic sounds of a city finally settling down after a hard day's work.

He picked up the pen. The smooth steel cylinder felt awkward between his fingers. He heard the binding crack and creak as he opened the journal for the first time. The blank, white pages gave him no clue as to what to write.

But his heart knew, somehow, what needed to be written and what had to be emptied from the angry place deep inside him.

His thoughts drew a scene in the center of the page: his father's tear-lined face engulfed in a shroud of flame and smoke, followed by his own stunning fall to the hay-strewn ground.

Josiah dropped the pen and stood up. The cover to the journal slowly closed itself. He squeezed his eyes shut, not wanting to relive that next terrible moment which still haunted him. His hands trembled.

He wanted to scream, wanted to punch a fist or throw a stone.

Three soft knocks broke the power of his memories. Josiah quickly wiped away his tears.

Toby opened the door and stuck his head inside. "Just wanted to say good night. You did some fine work today. And don't forget your prayers."

Josiah nodded. Toby smiled warmly and closed the door.

Tired but not ready to sleep, Josiah dragged the chair from behind the desk and placed it in front of the open window. Sitting down, he leaned forward and crossed his arms on the windowsill.

What happened after he had fallen from the loft leapt back into his thoughts. He had prayed so many times that God would take away all the memories of that night, terrible memories he had never shared with anyone.

But Heaven was like a vast dome of cold iron, impenetrable—echoing back his ardent requests, unanswered.

7

Wednesday morning began bright and cheery. Fresh from the Third Street Eatery breakfast, Toby, Angelina and Josiah arrived at the train terminal at nine o'clock. A gray, overcast sky had moved in with a threat of morning showers.

Toby stacked the fifth and last crate of books and handbills on the edge of the long platform beside the tracks. Josiah sat forward on one of the crates, his arms propped on his knees.

"That does it," Toby said, pressing his hands into his back and arching. "Now we need to pray that Sam and Daniel will get these books and handbills into the hands God wants them in."

Daniel? Josiah looked up and thought back to his trip to the telegraph office with Angelina. Now he remembered the name. Daniel Sweetwater was the author of the book that Toby and he had finished printing earlier in the week—the book that filled the crates stacked all around them.

Angelina smiled confidently and placed her hand on Toby's forearm, then glanced at Josiah. "The Lord knows exactly which hearts need to hear Daniel's story. He'll make a way."

"Why do you have to go to Washington?" Josiah asked.

"To help Sam lobby Congress and make the anniversary of the Emancipation Proclamation a national holiday. But we're also promoting my father and Daniel Sweetwater's book.

"You'll get a chance to meet Daniel later this week. Remember the telegram? He'll be stopping over one night. Sam and Daniel are not only championing freedmen's rights, but also the rights of all the Indian nations. Daniel has lived a very special life for God. When Daniel speaks, it's hard not to listen."

Indians? Josiah wondered why Angelina and her father were mixing up issues of the freedmen and the Indians.

Angelina continued. "Sam's also trying to secure land for Daniel's work in Shawnee Mission, Kansas. The Shawnee reservation there is severely overcrowded. My father has a soft spot for the Shawnee. Part of his growing-up years was spent there. My grandfather, Eli, was the son of a Shawnee woman. He published a Methodist newspaper where Sam helped out as a young man. That's how he first got into the publishing business."

The shriek of a steam-whistle brought Josiah to his feet. The train puffed into view as it rounded a bend in the tracks.

"So," Angelina said happily, "I guess I'm just about off. Daniel will arrive later this week before meeting Father and me in Washington. We should all be back on Tuesday. If there are changes, I'll wire you the details."

The corners of Toby's lips edged upward. "Josiah and I will be standing right here waiting for you all."

Angelina wrapped her arms around their shoulders and gave them a big hug. The engine and its cars slowed to a stop beside the long platform. Porters appeared on the steps to each car. The crowd that had quickly gathered now narrowed into lines waiting to board. Toby flagged a porter and pointed to the crates.

To Josiah's surprise, Angelina drew close. She put her hand on his shoulder. Concerned eyes searched his. She leaned forward and planted a small kiss on his cheek.

"You take care, Josiah. Keep your chin up. And don't forget what we talked about yesterday afternoon."

Josiah stuffed his hands way down into his pockets and nodded—a little embarrassed and a little confused, not really sure what she wanted him to remember.

By the time the train carrying Angelina had steamed over the bridge at Ellard's Crossing on its way to Washington, Toby had directed Angelina's buggy to the west end of town.

Josiah looked from the street sign to his boss. "You took the wrong turn. Freedom Press is the other way!"

Toby snapped lightly on the reins and picked up their pace. "We're not going back yet. We need to visit Honest Abe's Freight Company. Last evening, while we helped remove those dead mules, I asked the driver a few questions. Found out why he flipped his car. He told me that a man on horseback bolted into the intersection and stopped in the center of the street. Who'd do a dangerous thing like that? Makes no sense! There's more to this, I'm sure."

Josiah just listened. As they turned another corner, Honest Abe's shop came into view. The owner had turned an old arcade and bathhouse into a freight car terminal with two huge, open-bay doors facing the street.

Toby pulled over to the curb. As they climbed down from the buggy, a heavyset freedman with ebony skin and short-cropped black hair stepped up onto the sidewalk and greeted them. A stubby cigar protruded from the corner of his mouth.

"What'ya need?" the man asked grumpily. Josiah noticed that his cigar was not lit.

Toby extended a hand. The man shook it cautiously.

"The name is Sykes, Toby Sykes. My partner and I run the Freedom Press, over on Chestnut Street, just a few doors down from the Ledger Building. We publish the *Freedman's Journal*."

The man chewed on his cigar, his squinty eyes moving from Toby to Josiah and back. He looked puzzled. "*Freedman's Journal*, huh? I've read it. You two seem to run a decent shop."

Josiah glanced nervously at his boss.

Toby let loose with a hearty laugh. "This here's Josiah, our soon-to-be apprentice compositor. My partner is Sam MacDonald."

The man's eyes lit up at the name. "MacDonald, you say. Yes, I remember now. He wrote a fair piece about my brother's new grocery last year. C'mon in."

Josiah followed Toby through the wide bay door. The interior of the arcade had been converted into a garage housing a dozen cars.

They turned and entered a narrow office.

The man walked around behind the desk and sat down. "Sorry for the cold shoulder, but Honest Abe Johnson is in no mood to be talkin' to strangers this morning. Bein' your shop's near the *Ledger*, you know I lost another car yesterday afternoon—second car this week. I'm worried City Hall might take some action against my business. Fortunately, the cargo was rough lumber or I'd be in even deeper trouble with my customer."

Josiah chuckled inwardly. This was Honest Abe? From the sound of the name, he had figured the freight company had been named after Lincoln!

"That's exactly why we're here," Toby explained. "To see if we can help. Can't do much about City Hall. But a little good press in Friday's edition of the *Freedman's Journal* could go a long way with public opinion. Besides, I did a bit of freight car drivin' in my younger days, enough to buy my freedom."

Abe nodded appreciatively as he tossed his gnawed cigar into a brass spittoon in the corner. Josiah cringed at the thought of what might be piled inside the spittoon.

"Then you'll appreciate what I'm goin' to show you," he said, picking a piece of tobacco from his teeth as he talked, "I don't believe either of 'em was accidents. Come with me."

Toby and Josiah followed Abe out into the garage. They passed by workers hitching up teams of mules to three different freight cars. Josiah felt a strong urge to pinch his nose. He was glad that he did not have the job of shoveling out that garage and washing it down every day!

To Josiah's relief, Abe opened a door at the back of the garage and they went outside.

"Now I know my boys tend to drive a little fast—tell me whose freight drivers don't! But there's something more goin' on. Let me show you."

He directed them to two stacks of four wheels that were leaning against the back of the garage. "Saved these from my two wrecked cars." He pulled the top wheel away from the stack.

"Look here," he said, pointing a stubby finger at the hub. "What d'ya see?"

Josiah leaned forward and studied the wheel, then stepped back. Toby took his turn, then answered. "Looks like a hub."

Josiah nodded.

The freight company owner smiled smugly. "That's what I thought you'd say. Take a closer look—see that?" He drew his finger along a narrow cut that led to a major break in the hub.

Toby and Josiah nodded.

"I can't prove it," Abe continued, "but I don't think that break's natural. In that other stack is a second wheel with a break just like this one."

Toby rested his hands on his hips and scrunched his mouth thoughtfully. "Hard to prove something like that, isn't it?"

Frustration creased Honest Abe's face. "You bet. Somebody could've sawed my hub, then slapped a little mud over top to hide his dirty work. With a cut like that, sooner or later that wheel had to go. If there's stress put on it—like havin' to avoid someone stoppin' in the street right in front of your car—bam! The wheel pops and the load gets dumped on the ground. What's worse—you'll likely lose a mule or two!"

Toby turned to Josiah. "What do you think, son?"

Josiah looked back at the damaged hub. He did not know enough about wheels to make a sound judgment. What stuck out in his mind was Waylan Vestry stepping out from the crowd and offering the driver his long-barreled Colt.

"I suppose it could happen."

"I think it's worth a column in Friday's edition," Toby said with conviction. "If I have the time, I'd like to include a drawing. This on top of the freedmen accused of shooting those firemen at the warehouse is going to turn a lot of white folk against us. Doesn't matter if it's true or not."

Honest Abe extended his hand. "Much appreciated. You gotta believe me. I'm goin' to warn my boys about speedin'. Good folks put up a lot of hard-earned money to get this business goin'. I sure don't want to let them down. Freedmen tryin' to better themselves have enough trouble as it is."

8

Just before Adam entered the Public Ledger Building on his way to work, he glanced at the State House. He could see the old maple tree where he and his gang had finally cornered Josiah. Adam knew if he wanted to renew a relationship with Christine, he could not let his incident with Josiah remain unsettled. Besides, his anger in the heat of the moment had made him appear to be a different kind of person than he actually was.

Still, he had unleashed those hurtful words right in front of her. Would she forgive him? He would have to apologize to her, that was for sure.

After that?

Maybe he would also get a chance to make up to the kid, Josiah, in some small way, without his gang or his father finding out about it. That would impress Christine a lot, and it would also clear his conscience some.

The thought of becoming like his father made Adam even more uncomfortable with what he had done. Adam pushed open the glass doors to the Public Ledger Building and hurried inside.

This morning his father had left for the office much earlier than normal. The sound of the side door opening beneath his bedroom window had pulled Adam from his bed. Leaning against the window sill, he had watched his father head down their cobbled walk toward the street in the gray, dawn light. Waylan had held his head high, his strides long and confident—full of purpose.

In the past several months, his father had left home for a growing number of early morning and late night meetings. For what purpose? Certainly not the paper's. His father commanded legions of employees who worked three shifts around the clock.

And then there was the new lodge his father had joined. Adam had never before seen his father show much interest in the Masons.

Why, he was not sure, but Adam had a disturbing feeling that there were connections he was missing and that his father was up to something no good.

Josiah thought about Abe's last remark as the buggy rambled back toward the Freedom Press. And he could not stop seeing the image of Vestry emerging from the crowded corner, arm extended and pistol in hand. The look on his face had not been one of remorse. He had seemed to actually enjoy watching the discouraged driver shoot his injured mules, one by one. Poor Abe. Not everyone wanted him or his business to succeed.

The buggy came to a stop. Josiah looked up. To his surprise, they had not returned to the shop. Instead, Toby had parked against the curb by the grassy square behind the State House where Adam and his friends had cornered him the day before. The Public Ledger Building was across the street to their left.

"I know," Toby interjected as he hopped down from the buggy. "I took the wrong turn, but only by one block."

Josiah jumped down and followed Toby up the sidewalk that ran behind Congress Hall and the State House.

Toby stopped by the back corner of the State House and pointed up at the tower. "There she is, the Liberty Bell."

Josiah squinted and eyed the bell. What was his boss up to?

"Once in a while," Toby continued, "I just need to stop by and remind myself why Sam and I decided to settle down here. Philadelphia's always been a city of hope for men like Honest Abe Johnson and me. Once in a while we get knocked down to our knees, but we'll claw and fight to get back on our feet and keep doing what's right in God's eyes."

Toby lowered his head and stared straight at Josiah. "The other day, you got knocked down, too. I saw what it did to you. Don't try covering up your feelings. That scrub on your head's half-healed, but I know your heart tells a different story. You've seen hatred close up, hatred that can steal a man's life. If I were you, I'd fear that hatred in your heart a lot more than I'd fear what Adam Vestry or his gang might do. When it's all said and done, your duty to God is to do what's right in His eyes and let Him handle the rest."

Josiah wanted to look away, but something in Toby's gaze kept him from moving his eyes or turning his head. Toby reached into the inside pocket of his coat and pulled out a narrow, five-inch-long box.

"Josiah, you know you're not the first man who's had to deal with anger and injustice and the temptation to hate. Now I understand why I believe the Lord wanted me to give you this new pen. Sam and I gave you a journal that I bet's still as blank as the day I bound it. You need to start putting your life down just the way it happens—all of it. Write it for God to read and nobody else: what's been good and what's been bad; what's been fair and what's been unjust."

Toby's broad smile returned. "Cost me a pretty penny, too, so take good care of it. Now you can put that old, chipped gray one in the trash."

Josiah accepted the small box. Unexplainably, a reply slipped from his mouth. "OK. I'll try writing some."

Toby's face seemed to shine. His happy expression stopped Josiah from taking back his promise.

Toby patted Josiah on the shoulder. "I've got only one run slated today and I plan to start it shortly after lunch. I've decided to work up a sketch from Honest Abe's for this week's paper. Your time's your own until I return. You deserve it."

Josiah forced the best smile he could. "Thanks."

Toby waved and headed down the walk toward the buggy.

* * *

After leaning back against the maple tree that saved him from a thorough beating, Josiah turned the box over and over in his hands. His gaze rose to the fluttering leaves, then to the Liberty Bell atop the State House. Then he folded his arms across his chest. A breeze rustled the leaves above his head.

Though he wished he had not promised Toby he would start writing, he could not stop the smile that resulted from the generous gift.

Josiah opened the box. His mouth fell open as he removed the pen.

The swirling colors in the mother-of-pearl inlay made the pen sparkle in the light. The shiny brass nib caught the sun and flashed golden. The shank felt so smooth between his fingers. It was really a fine piece of workmanship!

As he started to return the pen to the box, he noticed a thin, folded strip of paper in the bottom. He pulled the strip out and unfolded it. Toby had penned him a short note!

> *Let us hear the conclusion of the whole matter: Fear God, and keep his commandments: for this is the whole duty of man. For God shall bring every work into judgment, with every secret thing, whether it be good, or whether it be evil. Eccl. 12:13-14*

Josiah knew the words came from the Bible. He chewed lightly on his lower lip and thought about the verses for several seconds, then stuffed the paper into his pocket. He was not quite sure what Toby and God were trying to say.

Unless . . . . Suddenly, all Josiah could think about was that dark summer night ten years ago. He sprang to his feet and glared first at the Liberty Bell, then up to the clear blue sky.

Would God really bring every work into judgment?

Those three bounty hunters had never been caught—would never be caught! How was God going to make them pay?

Josiah swallowed hard and blinked tears from his eyes. "What kind of God are you?"

Hardly aware of the traffic, Josiah ran across the street and started down the sidewalk toward the Freedom Press.

He unlocked the shop door and went inside. From the silence, he knew that Toby had not yet returned from Honest Abe's.

Josiah planted himself on a stool behind the front counter and laid his pen down in front of him. How could Toby possibly think that writing in his journal was going to help?

He dug the note out of his pocket and pondered the verse again. If God really cared about justice and doing what was right, then he should do something about it! How could freedmen ever hope to make their way with powerful men like the bounty hunters who killed his parents or with Waylan Vestry against them?

Hearing the sound of the rear door opening and closing at the end of the hall, Josiah climbed down from the stool.

A voice called out. "I'm back!"

Toby appeared in the doorway to the hall, sketchbook in hand. His eyes moved from Josiah's troubled face to the pen and the note on the counter, then back to Josiah.

Josiah picked up his pen and the note, then hurried past Toby into the hall.

Toby turned and placed his sketchbook on the layout table as Josiah climbed the stairs toward their living quarters.

"I'll need you back down here in five minutes sharp. We have a lot of work to do this afternoon."

Exactly five minutes later, Josiah returned empty-handed and silent, the expression on his face as stiff and wooden as a seasoned plank.

9

Waylan Vestry loomed over his wide cherry desk. He pulled a gold pocket watch from his vest and checked the time: eleven fifty-eight.

He breathed deeply, the lines around his eyes and mouth deepening. Snapping the watch shut, he slipped it back into his vest pocket.

Across the street from his second floor office in the Public Ledger Building, he could see Congress Hall, the State House and the Liberty Bell. Everyone agreed that his office was the best on the floor, replete of luxury and tradition.

His pride and joy, a suit of shining medieval armor with a brilliant red-plumed helmet, stood against the wall opposite his desk. On either side of the suit of armor were matching red velvet armchairs. Three large oil paintings on the wall behind his desk revealed his love for expensive art. He deserved the best; after all, he was the manager of the paper's national desk.

However, at this moment, tomorrow's edition of the *Ledger* was the last thing on his mind.

He opened the door to his office and stepped into the hall. His guests were right on time. Two tall men wearing dark-gray suits and vests came walking up the stairs across from his office door.

Noting their serious faces, Waylan straightened his shoulders, then casually stroked the hair on the right side of his forehead, bringing his fingers around behind his ear. He hoped he had executed the hand signal correctly. He wanted to impress these two influential men from the Ku Klux Klan.

As the men approached his office, the man on the right ran his hand through the hair on the left side of his head in an identical motion. The Ku Klux Klan hailing sign worked just like the coded telegram explained it would!

Waylan restrained showing pleasure even though he enjoyed the thrill of secrecy, code words, and covert hand signals.

"Mr. Crawford and Mr. Jennings, please step inside. It's a pleasure to meet you gentlemen." Vestry closed the door and continued talking. "I hope the trip from Tennessee was a pleasant one."

The square-jawed man called Crawford placed his bowler on the hat tree by the door. Jennings did the same. Without answering, they crossed the room. Jennings sat down stiffly in the first armchair beside the suit of armor. Crawford stood in front of the second chair, hands behind his back.

"The trip north," Crawford bellowed in a surly, southern accent, "was abominable. Your coloreds are rude and disrespectful."

Jennings concurred. "And, accordin' to this morning's paper, your city's freight car drivers are dangerously out of control."

Waylan chuckled. "I've got local officials looking closely at the situation. One more mishap and that freight company will be out of business. My men did a good job of setting up the accident."

Crawford broke into a wide, crooked smile. His pale eyes brightened slightly. "I see. And the warehouse that burned down, your men started that fire, didn't they?"

Waylan let go with a deep chuckle. "Once we got those coloreds drinking, everyone knew a disaster was about to happen—like a lantern overturning and starting a fire. They even thought they did it! The flames got so big so fast the fire company didn't have a chance to save the warehouse."

"Then I'm glad I can report that our plan is working," Crawford replied. "The Great Grand Cyclops will be pleased. He believes the government is about to take action against the Klan. We believe that we need to get the public, ordinary citizens, back on our side. Mr. Jennings and I agree."

Jennings nodded. "All of the Grand Cyclops agree, from Texas to Alabama to Virginia. We must convince the average white man that these so-called freedmen aren't worthy of that freedom."

Crawford made a fist. "The federal government in Washington has sold out to the devil, the Republicans and the coloreds. The public must see that the Klan is our nation's last, shining hope for chivalry, humanity, mercy and patriotism."

The Klansman's southern drawl and fiery words stirred Waylan's heart. Soon, he would have the official support he needed to start his own Ku Klux Klan den, his own Invisible Empire, right here in Philadelphia!

In the South, nighttime cross burnings were commonplace. Blacks found themselves beaten, whipped and lynched where Southern judges and juries were sympathetic to the Klan. Here in the North it did not work that way. At least, not yet.

But soon that would change. All it would take is a few more burned down warehouses, a riot here and there, and a white church set on fire—all blamed on local coloreds.

And then he, Waylan Vestry, would rise behind the scenes to become the first Grand Cyclops north of the Mason-Dixon Line!

Waylan walked over to the window and clasped his hands together.

"Gentlemen, the following eight days must be carefully staged. The events will occur just prior to next week's Emancipation Proclamation celebration. To coordinate our plans, I've brought in a special agitator from Maryland. With his help, I'm going to bring down that troublesome Freedom Press."

Jennings nodded his approval.

"MacDonald's the owner, right?" Crawford asked, after a brief pause.

"That's right." Waylan stepped to his desk. "But it's not only MacDonald who's a problem, it's his daughter and his colored shop manager Sykes, too. Nothing but trouble, every one of them. And it's not just his paper—their young apprentice, Josiah Washington, got into a scrap with my son just yesterday, right across the street. Adam gave that former slave boy a lot less than he deserved."

Crawford turned his head, his eyes narrowing. "How old's the boy?"

Waylan shrugged. "Around fifteen, sixteen. I'm not really sure. Why do you ask?"

"Just some old family business that needs tending to, that's all," Crawford replied with a crooked smile and his voice trailing off. "Been ten years."

The desire for revenge surged through Waylan's blood so hotly that he ignored Crawford's suddenly happy expression and cryptic answer.

His confidence growing stronger by the moment, Waylan pulled out a map of the city showing his plans for the next stage of his plot. He would pull the Freedom Press and everybody who worked there into his web and then blast them all out of business and out of Philadelphia—for good!

10

Standing on the front steps of a tobacconist shop opposite the Public Ledger Building, Adam stared across the street at the Freedom Press. From the shop, he could easily see through the print shop's large front window. Toby and Josiah were working with one of their tabletop presses.

The young man tucked the bag of tobacco under his arm, then slipped his cap back onto his head with a short tug. His father's big six-cylinder Hoe rotary presses, with their mechanized cutters and folders, could print 74,000 daily copies of the *Public Ledger*. At the Freedom Press, Toby and Josiah would have to slave ten hours a day all week long to match just one day's output from the *Ledger*'s presses! How could their two-cent Friday paper ever hope to compete with the *Ledger*'s twelve-cent per week daily? The odds were stacked against them.

Adam darted across the street right behind an omnibus loaded with sour-faced women from the Temperance Society. He slowed down as he reached the sidewalk in front of the Ledger Building.

He looked up. Six stories tall and a block wide, the sheer size of the building spoke of the newspaper's growing influence in Philadelphia.

Adam entered the Public Ledger Building. He made his way toward the center stairs. Reporters, pressmen, compositors, and printer's devils with their ink-stained hands and arms criss-crossed the lobby. He bolted up the stairs to the second floor and turned the corner to the right.

Slipping off his cap, he approached his father's office with the bag of chewing tobacco in hand. He read the nameplate on the closed door: Waylan T. Vestry, Manager, National Desk.

He pressed his ear to the door. Yes, he could hear his father's deep voice. Without considering the consequences, Adam quietly cracked open the door and peeked inside. After all, he did have that bag of tobacco his father had asked him to bring over.

Waylan stood in front of the window, his face tense and his arms motioning vigorously. A large map of the city lay draped across the corner of his roll-top desk. A dozen locations on the map were marked with thick circles of red ink.

One of his father's visitors sat in an armchair by the suit of armor; the other stood nearby. Adam studied their faces. He had never seen either of them around the office before.

Waylan continued. "We cannot allow the Freedom Press to use their weekly paper to keep pumping Republican poison into the minds of Philadelphians. They must be stopped, and I suggest we must be the ones to stop them."

The square-jawed man who stood nodded in agreement. One side of his mouth snaked up into an evil smile.

Vipers! That was it! That's what they reminded Adam of: cold-blooded predators who would sink their fangs right into you without a pinch of regret.

Adam cringed, pulled his head away from the crack and silently closed the door. What were they planning?

Adam leaned against the wall and took a deep breath. When it came to freedmen, his father had become two different people. In public, Waylan Vestry showed himself a model citizen, trumpeting freedmen's rights; but at home, his disgust for Toby Sykes and the Freedom Press clouded his face like a twisted mask.

And now, right in his own newspaper office, he was meeting and making ominous plans with unfamiliar men of obviously questionable character! And why the map of Philadelphia and the dark red circles?

As he backed away from the door, sadness cast a shadow over his heart. Shame crept along his cheeks and neck. Though he could blame the incident with Josiah behind the State House on the heat of the moment and on embarrassment, Adam now realized that there had been something else working in him that day, something worse than mere pride. During the few seconds before Christine had arrived to defend Josiah, he had felt a sudden, pleasurable surge of power when he took advantage of someone who could not really fight back.

Adam rubbed the back of his neck. It didn't take much of a leap to imagine what his father and his new friends with their evil smiles were planning had something to do with that same kind of selfish power.

The afternoon and evening rushed by for Josiah in a blur of folding, stacking and boxing. Now, after a late dinner with Toby, he leaned forward in his chair and propped his elbows on the window sill.

Cool night air brushed his face. The scattered glow of yellow lamp light from the windows of the buildings across Sixth Street revealed which shop owners lived above their stores.

Behind him, the open journal, his new pen, and a capped ink well beckoned from the desk in the corner of his dark room. Though he had not forgotten Toby's advice, he had not yet acted on it, despite the quiet urgings of a small, but encouraging voice from somewhere inside his conscience.

Josiah listened to the sounds of the night. Dogs barked noisily in the alley behind the Freedom Press. Three white men held a heated conversation on the sidewalk in front of a tavern a half block way. Josiah could hear enough to know they were talking about Honest Abe. They were mad at Honest Abe, mad at his reckless freedmen drivers, and mad about the mules being shot in the head directly in front of the State House.

The blood in Josiah's cheeks burned hot. He wanted to yell loudly enough for the men to hear, "Someone fooled with Abe's wagon wheels—someone like you!" or, "Abe's a better man than all of you put together!"

His emotions smoldered like coals in an iron stove, with a fiery red core barely hidden beneath a powdery covering of ash.

Josiah looked back over his shoulder at his desk and open journal.

He sucked in a deep breath, turned back to the window and stared up at the silvery band of stars across the sky. One of the three men standing outside the tavern was shouting. The dogs began barking even more loudly.

Josiah scraped back his chair, jumped to his feet and slammed the window shut.

He turned and climbed into bed. He grabbed his pillow, folded and pounded it with his fists over and over and over again until his arms ached.

Josiah rolled onto his side, exhausted. Ignoring the small voice a second time, he held back his hurt, shut his mouth, and closed his eyes. Prayer, like writing in his journal, was not something he wanted to do.

Sleep came eventually, and with it, the nightmares.

11

Waylan Vestry's second early morning meeting in a row had progressed smoothly. He leaned back in his armchair and ran his hand slowly down the iron gauntlet on the armor standing beside him.

Now that Crawford and Jennings were on a train to New York, he could get on with business. As much as he wanted the power that came with the position of running his own KKK den, working with men like Crawford and Jennings was no pleasant task.

They lacked manners and used brute force instead of clear thought and good planning. They refused to work with coloreds in any way. In that regard, Crawford was dead wrong. Coloreds, particularly angry former slaves, could be extremely useful if they were controlled properly.

Like his new hired hand, Lucius Morris, a half-breed from Maryland. Lucius' three older brothers had been lynched by drunken Confederate soldiers shortly after Lee's surrender at Appomattox—justly or unjustly, it did not matter. What mattered was how Lucius was anxious for revenge.

Waylan looked up and studied the dark eyes and angular, chestnut face of the muscular young man who leaned against his desk. He liked the expression on Lucius' face. Waylan knew that Lucius' anger could be channeled as long as Lucius did not discover he was actually working for the KKK! Playing on the fears and frustrations of an angry colored like Lucius—and the other coloreds Lucius was busy recruiting—and using them as sacrificial pawns was a very dangerous game.

But play the game he would! The stakes were high but so were the rewards of power and prestige.

Waylan grinned. Lucius actually believed that he and his recruits were joining an organization to improve freedmen's rights!

Lucius turned and studied the map spread open across the desk. His eyes narrowed. "How reliable are your sources about the Klan?"

"Very reliable. As a newspaper man, I have many contacts."

"I still find it hard to believe that the Ku Klux Klan would attempt to move into the North," Lucius said, his eyes flashing. "Why not just publish their names? The public outcry against them would be overwhelming."

"Yes, and that's what I'm afraid of. We don't need to stir up everybody with a rip-roaring battle cry. The last thing Philadelphia needs is a war between the races. No, we need to send the Klan the kind of message they understand: an eye for an eye and a tooth for a tooth.

Waylan pointed a thick finger at Lucius. "That's why I hired you. Besides, didn't the Klan string up your three brothers and burn down your house? This is your chance for real justice."

Lucius hung his head, closing his eyes.

Vestry watched the pain etch Lucius' face before he continued. "My contacts in Kansas told me about your work with John Brown before the war."

Lucius nodded, his hands contracting into fists.

"Good," said Waylan, considering his next lie. "Then we have a common goal. We must defeat the Klan before they can gain a foothold in Philadelphia."

"Nothing would make me happier, Mr. Vestry."

Waylan stood up. "I'll inform my contacts that you'll begin putting our plan in motion right away. They're very close to finding out the names of the Klansmen who organized the den. What could be a better reason for freedmen to take action?"

Morris shrugged. "Wanting freedom and doing something about it are two different things. Josiah and the others, they've got to believe in me and in the goals of our organization. Standing up against the Klan is a frightful thing, but if we have the right information and we're patient, I believe that we can be successful."

Vestry's grin broadened as he crossed the office to his desk. He picked up the map of the city and folded it as he spoke. "All right, let's get on with it, then."

He almost patted Lucius on the shoulder, but caught himself just in time. With a simple nod of his head, he dismissed his hired hand.

Adam peered around the corner in the hall as a freedman casually closed the door to his father's office. With his vest jacket draped over one arm and a worn Panama hat in hand, the freedman walked confidently toward the stairs.

Adam rubbed his chin. An hour ago, his father had excused himself from breakfast at home to attend an important early morning meeting with the mayor at City Hall.

Acting on a hunch, Adam had followed a few minutes behind only to discover that his father was having another secret meeting at his office. And the man he had met with this morning was certainly not the mayor of Philadelphia!

His father's office door opened a second time.

Adam peeked around the corner. Coat and hat in hand, his father closed the door to his office. He jiggled the doorknob to make sure it was locked, then glanced toward the stairwell.

Quickly pulling back, Adam hoped that his father would not turn and come his way. How could he possibly explain why he was hiding around the corner from his father's office? At this time of the morning, it would look like spying, no matter how he spun the story.

Adam sighed a breath of relief as his father's footsteps faded in the opposite direction.

Without warning, the office door behind him opened abruptly.

A short, balding man wearing a white shirt with his sleeves rolled up, charged into the hall, nearly bowling Adam over. The man recognized Adam and began muttering to himself.

Adam raised his hands to apologize, then lowered them as the man scurried on down the hall. Adam quickly backed around the corner toward his father's office, pulling a key ring from his back pocket. He offered a silent prayer of thanks that his father never found out that he had made a duplicate key.

The door unlocked with a dull click. Adam slipped inside and quietly closed the door behind him.

He looked around the room. Somewhere in the office was a map of Philadelphia, a map marked with red circles—and he was going to find it!

Over his mug of steaming coffee, Toby watched Josiah use his fork to roll his hard-boiled egg around the flapjacks on his plate.

"You've got to eat something," Toby suggested with his regular morning growl. "We worked real hard yesterday and I suspect we're gonna work real hard again today. A young man like you should fill his plate and start the day off right."

"I'm not hungry." Josiah set the fork down beside the plate and stared absentmindedly at the egg.

Toby shook his head slowly, then sipped his coffee. "Isn't right. A man's—."

"There's a lot that isn't right," Josiah interrupted sullenly.

"You're right about that," Toby agreed, softening his expression. "Come to think of it, I'm not so hungry now, myself." He pushed his coffee cup and unfinished plate of flapjacks into the middle of the table.

Surprised, Josiah peered at Toby.

The print shop manager rose from his chair and carried the dishes from the table to the sink.

"Maybe if we work extra hard, we can finish early and take Angelina's buggy down to the river for a little evening fishing. I just heard about a place where foot-long bass jump straight up out of the water. What do you say? Do we have a deal?"

Josiah weighed Toby's offer. "You mean it?"

"In the two weeks you've known me, have I ever said something I didn't mean?" Toby asked in the most serious voice he could muster.

Josiah beamed. "You've got yourself a deal."

Adam's expression darkened. He could not find the map. He had looked carefully at the papers in the roll-top desk and shuffled through the file drawers. He checked the cubbyholes and the small, two-shelf bookcase next to the desk. He even looked under the cushions of the side chair.

"Blast it all!" he said, swiveling around in his father's chair.

Where could the map be? Maybe his father had folded it up, stuck it in his coat pocket and taken it with him.

Adam popped open his pocket watch and glanced at the time, then pushed himself from the chair.

Today was an early shift and apprentices had to be on time. His superintendent would start hollering if he was even one minute late—quotas, quotas, quotas!

Frustrated, Adam took one last look around the room. Had his father taken the map with him?

He left the room and locked the door, then sprinted up the stairs to the third floor. As soon as he had composed his quota of 5,000 ems—letters, numbers, special typesetting symbols or punctuation marks—the rest of the day was his own.

Such were the rewards of the fastest compositors who earned the informal but honored title of Swift!

The first run of Friday's *Freedman's Journal* passed quickly for Josiah. By 1 p.m., Toby had printed slightly over five thousand copies, while Josiah had folded and stacked the thousand that would be shipped early tomorrow on a predawn train to Washington, New York, Boston and a half dozen other cities.

As he worked, Josiah glanced at the headlines above each column on the three-column page. The backside of the paper was broken down into even more sections. Seemed like Sam and Toby had something to say about most every topic, from education to child labor legislation to civil liberty law suits.

And just as Toby promised, he had featured a short article about Honest Abe's Freight Company right on the front page. The article quoted Abe directly and included a promise that he would personally inspect every car before it left the garage.

"Josiah," Toby called, taking his foot off the treadle and stopping the press. "Looks like I'm about to run out of ink. Could you go grab a tin?"

"Yes, sir. Right away."

Toby resumed printing as Josiah crossed the room to a closet. He opened the door and looked inside, then scratched his head.

"We're out of ink."

Toby lifted his foot from the treadle and removed a freshly printed sheet from the tympan. He walked to the closet.

"We sure are. Guess I've got to send you down to Market Street Printing Supply. Get eight half-gallon tins and have George put them on our bill. Think you can handle it?"

Josiah smiled as he headed for the door.

After harnessing Angelina's filly to the buggy, Josiah jumped inside. Looking both ways, he pulled slowly out of the alley at Morton's Livery and Hack Stables onto Chestnut Street. As he passed by the Freedom Press, he waved to Toby who stood at the layout table composing a form for a wedding invitation.

Across the street in front of the tobacconist, a handsome freedman wearing a vest jacket and a Panama hat climbed onto his horse, then started down the street behind the buggy.

Josiah never glanced back. His wary eyes stayed focused left, front, and right, alert to pedestrians as well as to carriages and wagons on the busy street. A few minutes later, he pulled the buggy out from behind a crowded omnibus into the alley beside the printing supply house.

He jumped down and hurried inside. With only one customer in front of him, he was back out with the first two tins in no time. Three quick trips later, he placed the last of the tins securely behind the seat.

As he reached to untether the filly, a loud cry from the street caused him to spin around.

A burly wagoner driving an empty flatbed yanked sharply on the reins and brought his wagon to a rumbling halt.

"Watch where yer goin'! Market Street ain't no place for a stroll!" the wagoner barked angrily at a freedman standing in his path.

"Keep your speed down!" the man barked back, stooping to pick up his Panama hat.

The wagoner's face registered shock as the freedman remained where he was and carefully dusted his hat. Dropping the reins, he leapt from the flatbed onto the street. He was half a head taller than the freedman was.

The freedman eyed the approaching wagoner and held his ground. Josiah winced. Whatever contest the defiant freedman had planned ended with one blow. The wagoner's huge right fist sent him sprawling face-first into the street. The whole incident was over so fast that hardly a passerby took interest.

The freedman and his Panama hat found themselves deposited roughly at the edge of the alley near Josiah.

"Uppity colored!" the wagoner muttered behind his scowl as he returned to his flatbed.

Josiah helped the freedman to his feet and handed him his hat. The freedman's lip was split badly and was starting to swell.

"Thanks," he said, brushing off the front of his clothes and vest jacket.

"Your lip!" Josiah interrupted, pointing at his own as a guide.

The freedman gingerly rubbed his lip with the tip of his tongue. He squinted his eyes and pulled a handkerchief from his back pocket. He gently dabbed the blood away.

Their eyes met.

"Name's Lucius," the freedman offered, extending his hand.

"Josiah."

They shook hands.

"Wasn't right, what he did to you," Josiah said with a sigh.

"There's an awful lot that ain't right. Somethin' needs to be done," Lucius replied, holding the handkerchief to his lip.

A tingle slid down Josiah's spine. He nodded as the sourness in his heart boiled up. "But nothing's gonna change."

Lucius' eyes brightened momentarily. He breathed deeply and shrugged his shoulders. "Maybe, maybe not. But we can surely try."

Josiah untethered the filly. "How's that?"

"By banding together. You know, we're not just going to wake up one morning with pearly white skin."

Josiah laughed and climbed into the buggy. He shook his head at the thought of getting out of bed and discovering his body had changed colors!

Lucius continued. "Some of us are meeting tonight. Want to join us?"

Excitement stabbed at Josiah's stomach, followed by a little fear. "I don't know...."

The freedman slipped his hat into place. "Think about it. I'll be at the corner of Market and Delaware, down by the river, at midnight. There'll be four of us. We sure could use a fifth."

Josiah did not reply. Lucius grabbed the filly's bridle and guided her back into the street.

With a light snap on the reins, Josiah got the buggy moving. His heart was racing.

As he pulled away into the street, Lucius waved goodbye. "Remember. Midnight!"

Josiah did not look back.

12

Josiah placed the tins of ink inside the back hall. From around the corner he could hear Toby speaking.

He closed the rear door and grabbed two tins. He hurried down the hall and entered the workroom. He stopped just inside the door, his eyes popping wide open. His conversation with Lucius was, for the moment, forgotten.

Christine Thompson, with her cascade of strawberry blond hair, stood facing Toby.

Her father, the reverend, stood beside her. He was of medium height and round through the waist. His eyes were pale blue and beamed with honesty. His bushy eyebrows seemed to fold together when he smiled, with teeth as white as his clerical collar.

For a second, Josiah felt as if he were knee-deep in mud. His feet wouldn't move, forward or backward. Not sure what to do, he slowly set the ink tins down by the door.

The clink of the tins against the floor turned all eyes toward him. That was the last thing he wanted!

Toby nodded. "Josiah, glad you're back. Come on over here. Reverend Thompson wants to meet you."

Josiah's feet came unglued at last.

Reverend Thompson shook Josiah's hand. "Nice work, young man! Nice work. As good as any work the Freedom Press has done, wouldn't you say, Christine?"

"Yes, I agree," she said, stepping to Josiah's side and peering at the bulletin in her father's hand.

The sweet smell of soap reached Josiah's nose. He wanted to pull back from her, but there was nowhere to go. His back was already up against the printing press. Josiah blinked. If Adam somehow saw how closely she was standing to him. Well, he did not even want to think about it!

Reverend Thompson reached out and slapped Josiah happily on the shoulder. "Toby, I'm going to request that this young man compose all of our church materials. What do you say?"

Pursing his lips, Toby glanced from the reverend to Josiah. "I suppose that can be arranged, being that he's the only apprentice compositor I have to keep track of. He'll still have other, less-important duties to perform until Sam gets back and decides if we should hire a new printer's helper."

Toby's words filtered slowly through Josiah's brain. Could he believe what he just heard? Become an apprentice? He wanted to pinch himself on the arm to make sure he was not dreaming—or dead and gone to heaven! Being an apprentice meant a chance to learn a trade!

Toby put his hands on his hips and laughed. "Son, I made the decision a couple days ago. Sam'll back me up on this when he and Angelina return from Washington, I'm sure."

Christine nodded toward Josiah. "Congratulations!"

Reverend Thompson patted him firmly on the shoulder. "Well deserved, too!"

Josiah looked down. His feet shifted nervously, but he was trapped by the printing press behind him.

The reverend lifted the box of bulletins from the counter. "Christine, I think we should get going. I believe Josiah here is quite anxious to discuss the question of wages, now that he's been made such an outstanding offer. Oh, and by the way, can you deliver the rest of my order once it's ready?"

As Toby made a note, Christine looked Josiah straight in the face and smiled.

"Bye."

She turned and followed her father out the front door. She climbed into the carriage and waved as her father loaded the box behind the seat.

Toby and Josiah waved back. With the snap of the reins,

Reverend Thompson signaled the filly and edged the carriage into the street.

Josiah swelled with joy.

"All right, apprentice," Toby said in a serious tone that could not hide his own excitement. "We've got to get back to work if we want go fishin' a little later. I've got a feeling that those bass are gonna be jumpin' this evening."

"Yes, sir!" Josiah replied, crossing the room and grabbing the two tins of ink. He handed Toby one of the tins and carried the other one to the storage closet. As he put away the remaining tins, he could not deny that his initial feelings about Christine Thompson were changing rapidly.

The girl said what was on her mind, and she treated him like a friend.

Amazed but happy, Josiah, apprentice compositor for the Freedom Press, returned to his work, folding and stacking newspapers.

The warming winds that blew steadily up from the South made the prospect of evening fishing even more desirable.

Josiah chuckled and edged forward on the flat rock, lifting his fishing pole toward the river. In the two weeks he had been working at the Freedom Press, he could not remember having seen Toby treadle the press so swiftly. They had printed the Friday morning edition of the *Freedman's Journal* in record time. Toby had kept his word: the afternoon was for fishing.

He extended his long pole out into the shallows, dragging his line and a squiggling minnow beneath the leafy overhang of a nearby oak tree at the edge of the river.

Toby, hidden from view, was somewhere beyond the tree around a sharp bend in the riverbank, beneath the Old Stone Bridge.

Josiah stuck the pole between his knees, then leaned back and propped himself on his arms. The rock felt warm to his skin. A gentle breeze caressed his face. His gaze drifted out across the slow-moving river. His eyes began to close as his focus softened into a relaxing blur.

A soft plopping sound quickly brought Josiah back into a sitting position. He stared at the fading circles and sighed. He'd missed it! The bass were indeed leaping out of the water!

He jiggled his pole and watched the line sink as the minnow wiggled through the water.

"Three feet to the left and a bass will honor your dinner table tonight," spoke a rich, almost-melodious voice from behind him.

Startled, Josiah jerked lightly on his pole, then twisted around on the rock.

On the bank behind him, a black-haired man with a bronze face sat back in a comfortable squat on the heels of his leather-thonged moccasins, his arms resting over his knees. His long hair was pulled back from his smooth face and tied into a ponytail. He was dressed in tan leather pants of a style Josiah had only seen in books. He wore an open-collared, multicolored shirt without buttons. His smooth skin and dark hair made it hard to tell exactly how old he was.

But what grabbed Josiah's attention the most was the man's eyes: dark and strong, but gentle and honest.

"Quickly now," the man indicated with a subtle nod, "or the moment will pass."

Josiah obeyed and moved his pole an arm's length to his left. The line and minnow followed, moving from the shade of the overhanging oak into a patch of sun-dappled water.

Without warning, the tip of his pole arced downward into the water.

Josiah pulled upward on his pole just as Toby rounded the bend. "Look! I've caught a bass!"

Toby chuckled. "Well, Daniel, we're sure glad you found our note." He dropped to one knee as Josiah continued to work the struggling fish toward the shore. Toby reached out with his net and scooped up the bass as it splashed near the water's edge.

Josiah worked the hook from the bass's wide-open mouth,

then stood to face his benefactor, fishing net in hand. Unsure of exactly what to say, he stood up and said, "Thanks."

"You are welcome," Daniel Sweetwater replied, reaching his hand under the bottom of the net and lifting up. "And we are blessed. This large-mouth weighs at least three pounds. More than enough to feed three, wouldn't you say?"

From his place on the far side of the Old Stone Bridge, Adam leaned against the cool stones beneath the shadows of the oak trees lining the riverbanks. He watched Josiah and Toby lazily cast their lines and enjoy their fishing.

How long had it been since his father and he had fished? Four years, five? It seemed like a lifetime ago.

Adam folded his hands together and let his gaze drift down the river with the slowly moving currents.

Josiah and Toby had arrived earlier, laughing and joking, with fishing poles over their shoulders. They had been totally unaware that less than a half an hour before the Walnut Street gang had met right here on the bridge.

The meeting had been brief. In the end, his younger friends had left the bridge heading in one direction and Adam, the other. And Adam understood the split was more than a parting of ways. Something had changed. Pug, a sixteen-year-old and the Walnut Street Gang's second-in-command, had sensed the change, too.

"No hard feelings," Pug had said, sternly eyeballing the younger boys. "What a catch Christine Thompson would be! But she wouldn't put up with the likes of us, now would she? And you don't have the time, anyway."

The other gang members agreed.

The sound of a big fish thrashing through the water brought Adam out of his reverie.

He looked up and saw Josiah backing away and working his catch toward the riverbank. Toby bent down and scooped up a large-mouth bass with his net.

Behind Josiah and Toby, Adam watched a dark-skinned man slowly rise to his feet. Adam squinted his eyes, his fingers tapping lightly on the stone wall in front of him. The man was an Indian, all right, from his moccasins up to his long black hair pulled into a ponytail behind his head.

How about that! If the Indian went back to the Freedom Press with Toby and Josiah, Adam guessed his father would quickly discover that, too. Indian issues were another sore spot at the dinner table.

Adam grinned as Josiah hooked another minnow on his line. Toby placed the bass in a tall bucket on the bank. The Indian sat back on his heels, arms across his knees.

That would not be the only bass they would catch that evening, Adam mused as he pushed himself from the wall.

With an unseen tip of his hat to the men below, he turned and headed back across the bridge toward home.

Sitting at the round oak table in the kitchen area on the second floor of the Freedom Press, Josiah lifted a bite of bass to his mouth. Had fish ever tasted so sweet?

Daniel Sweetwater nodded as if he understood exactly what Josiah was thinking. Sitting a third of the way around the table to the right, Daniel reached for his glass.

"It has been many, many years since I have eaten such good fish. Perhaps it is merely a trick of my memory, but I am reminded of my boyhood home of Hiwassee."

Toby chuckled. "The Lord must be looking down from heaven and smiling on us, for Josiah to catch a bass like this here in the waters of Philadelphia!"

Josiah looked up. "Hi-wa-see? Where's that?"

Daniel took a sip of lemonade, then leaned back in his chair. "Hiwassee was a small village in Tennessee where my father began his call as a missionary pastor to the Cherokee people."

"But you're an—" Josiah began, but suddenly felt embarrassed to finish.

"An Indian. Yes." Daniel did not seem in the least offended. "By blood, I am Delaware. I now work with the Shawnee. But my heart is Cherokee, will always be Cherokee."

Daniel's eyes narrowed almost imperceptibly, but Josiah could sense the change in the tone of his voice.

"In the 1830's, it was not uncommon for members of one tribe to evangelize the members of another tribe. God works through his Spirit to reach peoples of every tribe and nation on this earth. And what better way than to use men of red skin to reach men of red skin?

"But I was barely a young man then, angered by the pains of injustice at the hands of white men. The troubles of my youth reached a climax in the winter of 1839, during a period of time known as the Indian Removal, on a bitter journey now remembered as the Cherokee Trail of Tears. I was sixteen."

Daniel's voice grew soft, almost to a whisper. A pale mist stole over his eyes. "In the span of a short five months, my entire world, all I drew comfort from, was lost. And I blamed it all on the white man. But in my heart, I was really angry with God. Only by God's grace do I have the honor to sit with you this night."

Toby sat forward and looked at Josiah. "Those crates of books that we sent with Angelina to Washington? They contained copies of Daniel and Sam's book, *Beneath the Sky of an Angry God*. Daniel and Sam are planning to hand out the book to key people in Washington. In just one generation, many have already forgotten the injustices suffered by the Indian nations."

Josiah listened and nodded. But inside, he wondered just how similar Daniel's situation was to his own. Josiah's ancestors had been seized from their village homes in Africa and packed into filthy and disease-ridden ships with less care than for cattle, and brought across the ocean to Charleston, South Carolina. Families were split apart and sold to plantation owners—like the man from Ellijay, Georgia, who had purchased his mother and father.

Toby pushed his plate into the middle of the table. The kitchen grew quiet. Only the tick of the wall clock was heard.

Daniel broke the silence. "Before dinner, Toby reminded me that you come from Ellijay. I, too, come from Ellijay."

Confused, Josiah set down his fork and knife. "Didn't you say you were from Hiwassee?"

Daniel nodded. "I was born in Hiwassee but raised as a young man about your age in Ellijay. During the Indian Removals, our entire town was taken from us. It was then sold to white families who were migrating westward from the East Coast. In one town not far from Ellijay, families were given no notice of their removal. They were driven from their dinner tables at gunpoint and loaded into wagons.

"My father and I lost our home, our fields, everything. At least we were able to take our personal belongings. I was so angry. Most of all, I hated the man who got our farm. And some years later, when I discovered our land and most of Ellijay had become part of Crawford's successful family plantation, the Devil tested my heart again."

Josiah's shoulders tingled down to his arms. His family had been owned by the only big plantation owner in Ellijay, a man the slaves called Master, but the whites called Mr. Crawford, or Jake.

Josiah looked at Toby, who stared down at his hands.

"But God has a way of turning evil into good. Evil men eventually fall into the very same traps they set for others. Men of violence die by violence."

Daniel paused, searching for the right words. "And for those of us who have suffered great injustices, if we are not careful, we can fall to the very same temptation. In the end, we become just like those we hate.

"Our lives are shaped by all the decisions we make. While I'm off to Washington City, I'm leaving in Toby's keeping the Bible that once belonged to my father and a knife given to me by an old frontiersman.

"The Bible and knife speak of the two-fold cord that is in every man—and in our nation, as well. When we choose God's way, we strengthen the good inside us. But when we choose our own way, we start down a path that leads only to pain and great suffering."

Josiah was too stunned to reply. He fiddled with the bass and the roasted potatoes on his plate, but his hunger had vanished. Instead, images of the burly, mustached plantation owner and his own family's harsh life as slaves came back to fill his thoughts and press once again upon his heart.

Later that evening, alone in his bedroom, Josiah thought about what Daniel had said. He moved away from the open window.

He could still feel the tension in his chest and stomach. The tightness drove away any desire for sleep. In the lamp glow on his desk beside his journal rested the book Daniel had given him after dinner: *Beneath the Sky of an Angry God*. He would not read it now. Maybe later.

He thought about the coincidence of their both living in Ellijay. But how similar were their lives? At least, Daniel's people still had their own lands—not their original lands, of course. Josiah understood that. But their lands were out west and out of the reach of white men and the U.S. Government.

After the war, some freedmen had been given small parcels of land for their own, but otherwise, their situations were different. Slaves had come from Africa; Indians lived in America. Slaves had been treated like chattel, less than beasts of burden. Josiah could still remember his parents explaining to him how a man could not legally hit his horse, but he could whip or even kill his slave!

No, Josiah decided. Their colors and their situations were different. And the decades that had passed since Daniel was a young man made the times now different, too.

Josiah returned to the window and stared out into the darkness above the buildings across the street. In just a few hours, Lucius and three other men would be meeting.

Midnight. That was the time and he was going to be there!

13

Josiah turned down his lamp and plunged the room into darkness. He opened his bedroom door. Gentle snoring from the room down the hall on the right told him that Toby slept soundly. He struck a match on the sole of his boot and lit the short candle.

He stepped into the hall and gently closed the door. With no other windows on this level, the candle would provide enough light to keep him from crashing into something. Cupping his hand around the candle, he passed quietly by Toby's room on the right and Sam's room on the left, now occupied by Daniel Sweetwater.

Entering the kitchen area, he stepped around the oak table and chairs where they had eaten their meal. To his right, the room opened to a three-sided alcove lined with tall bookcases. The candle cast a wavering yellow sphere on the book-laden shelves. Josiah glanced at the rows of Sam's and Toby's books, journals and personal effects. He could make out several items: a pipe rack, a pair of antique eye glasses, a three-quarter-inch iron ball from a canister round that had miraculously bounced off Toby's thigh at the battle at Shiloh during the Civil War, and a hand-blown vase of green glass.

As he continued around the room, his gaze passed over the top shelf of the middle bookcase. A Bible, lying flat on its side, jutted out over the edge of the shelf. And on top of the Bible was a leather-sheathed knife.

Josiah lifted the candle higher. A knife and a Bible? Then he remembered. His eyes darted momentarily down the hall.

Daniel's knife and Bible!

Josiah reached up and grabbed the knife. He set the candle on the bookshelf and studied the sheath. The old leather had been carefully preserved. He turned it over in his hand.

Josiah forced back a gasp.

Even in the low light, he could see that the sheath and knife handle were tooled with symbols: a bird's foot, a claw, and a turtle. With only a tiny pang of guilt, Josiah quickly strapped the sheath onto his belt. He would return it before Toby or Daniel discovered it missing.

Grabbing the candle, Josiah turned and started down the stairs to the back hall. He did not want to be late.

Three blocks southeast, Adam Vestry glanced at his pocket watch, turned the corner from Walnut onto Fifth Street, and entered the section of Philadelphia once known as Society Hill. The name made little sense. This part of town did not sit on a hill and it was not well-to-do. No one cared anymore that the Free Society of Traders once owned all of the land. The only thing that made Society Hill stand out from the rest of Philadelphia was its age: many of its homes were over a hundred years old.

Adam strolled down the moonlit sidewalk. His watch read a quarter to midnight. Only two blocks from home, he had made his curfew without a hitch—not that his father cared all that much, only when he had been drinking.

A couple of minutes later, Adam turned left into an alley that ran parallel to the street where he lived. The alley led to the gate at the rear of their property. From there he could enter the house through the back door off the kitchen and get to his own room without having to pass by his father's bedroom.

Six-foot-high stone walls lined the alley on either side. Tall, ancient chestnut trees arched high overhead, their full limbs deepening the shadows in the alley.

Twenty paces from the iron gate, Adam stopped. He heard a voice from behind the wall—his father's voice!

To his immediate right was a broken-down cart. As the gate creaked and swung open, Adam ducked into thick shadows behind the cart next to the wall.

Adam peeked out over the cracked buckboard.

Hand on the gate, his father stood with his back to the cart. A thin swath of moonlight filtered through the trees and reflected off his white hair. He spoke to a black man—the same black man Adam had seen leaving his father's office early that morning!

Adam fought back his surprise and listened.

"Lucius, your willingness to do what is right is worthy," Waylan continued, "An eye for an eye and a tooth for a tooth."

"I don't want praise, Mr. Vestry. I just want to root the Klan out of this city and out of this state. Well, it's time to go," Lucius explained, backing away down the street. "I'm due at Market and Delaware in ten minutes. My men will be waiting."

Waylan turned to the open gate, then paused. "Will the Washington boy be joining you tonight?" he asked as if it were an afterthought.

"Why, I suspect so, Mr. Vestry. Any reason you ask?"

"Just concern, that's all. But I'm sure you'll take good care of him."

Lucius nodded, then turned and hurried down the alley.

Waylan's tightly drawn lips curved slyly as he re-entered the gate and then closed it behind him.

From his place behind the cart, Adam watched as Lucius disappeared around a corner.

For several minutes, Adam just sat on his heels and rested against the rough stone wall. He rubbed his hands together and went over the strange conversation between his father and the black man called Lucius.

Adam shook his head. For the last couple of days, he'd had a growing suspicion that his father's lodge was not a lodge at all, and that his father was secretly working with the Ku Klux Klan!

But tonight's secret discussion seemed to tell an opposite

story, with his father congratulating Lucius for his plan to rid Philadelphia of the Klan.

Adam pushed himself to his feet.

The Klan in Philadelphia?

Nothing made sense! If his father really knew that the Klan was operating in Philadelphia and he wanted to stop it, all he would have to do is publish a front-page article in the *Ledger*. That would be really big news, important news that would sell thousands of additional copies of the paper and bring his father lots of public attention. And his father never passed up an opportunity to gain money or prestige.

No. His father was up to something big, something that linked his meeting with Lucius this morning and his meeting yesterday with the shifty Southerners. And all of the meetings had to be part of a plan—a plan detailed by a map marked with circles of bright red ink.

His search for that map in his father's office in the Public Ledger Building had proved fruitless. But his father had an office at home, too, in his study.

With eyes gleaming, Adam walked around the broken cart, silently opened the gate and slipped inside.

A half-hour later, Adam returned the small key to the porcelain snuffbox. He spun away from the fireplace, then looked one last time around his father's plush study. Bright moonlight from the two tall windows on his left painted the room and its furnishings with a pale, silvery sheen.

Adam had used the small, well-hidden key to open the locked desk opposite the windows. But the desk had not contained the map. Flipping through the two dozen books in the narrow bookcase by the desk proved futile as well. He carefully looked behind the three paintings on the far wall for secret enclosures, but found only the same wallpaper that decorated the rest of the room.

Adam leaned against the mantle and crossed his arms. He had also checked the pockets of his father's overcoat hanging on the hall tree in the foyer. Nothing there either.

Then where did his father keep that blasted map?

Adam shook his head and yawned. Enough was enough for one day. He crossed the study, opened the door a crack, and peeked down the main hall. The house was dark and quiet.

He left the study door fully open, just as he had found it.

Sooner or later he would find the map marked with red ink, just like he found the small key to his father's desk which had been hidden so cleverly in the empty snuff box on the mantle!

A sudden noise beside Adam's head startled him. The grandfather clock in the hall rang the first of twelve chimes.

Midnight.

Josiah, breathing hard from his six-block run and from worry knotting in his stomach, stood in the shadows of a warehouse at the corner of Market and Delaware.

He did not need to check his pocket watch to know what time it was. Block by block and minute by minute, he worked his way from street corner to street corner, the knot in his stomach growing tighter and tighter.

Josiah knew that his late-night venture put him at great risk. He could lose everything he valued, not just his good standing with Toby and Angelina, but now his new-found trade.

And yet . . . .

In the darkness beside the warehouse, resolve hardened Josiah's expression into a grimace. He knew he could not continue day after day and just do nothing. Men like Waylan Vestry did not let others stand in the way of their goals, and neither would he!

Josiah clenched his hands tightly into fists. He knew he could not escape his nightmares and his past. Lucius was right. The color of his skin would set him apart all the days of his life.

However, he could possibly change his future, and not only his future, but also the futures of many freedmen.

Movement caught Josiah's searching eyes.

Across the street, Lucius casually walked out of a dark alley onto Delaware Street. Behind him, three other men could be seen standing in the shadows.

Josiah breathed deeply, then stepped boldly away from the warehouse, his hand wrapped tightly around the knife strapped to his belt.

14

Lucius turned up the lantern. Yellow light filled the small room, casting dark shadows behind himself and the four men who stood with their backs to the closed door and shuttered windows. He set the lantern in the center of the only table in the room and motioned them toward the empty crates stacked along one side of the office.

"This warehouse office was given to us as a base of operations."

Josiah leaned back against a crate, his eyes narrowing. "Someone knows we're meeting here?"

"That's right," Lucius answered calmly.

Billy, twenty years old and a pipe fitter, uncoiled his muscular arms from over his chest. "You said there'd only be five of us."

"Yes I did. There are only five of us—on the front line. Behind us, however, are others who will help us with money and supplies. They provided this building."

Billy and Josiah exchanged glances with Horace and Harold, two brawny brothers with goatees who worked as cargo handlers for a nearby shipping company.

Lucius stepped to the side of the table and carefully chose his words. "I could recount the many injustices inflicted upon the freedmen of Philadelphia and other cities and towns in the North, but our own stories are painful enough.

"Three of my brothers were lynched for crimes they did not commit. Harold and Horace were separated from their parents and sold to a cruel master who beat them regularly for trying to learn how to read. Josiah's parents were burned alive in a barn by bounty hunters. And only Billy survived when an overcrowded boat capsized in a rain-swollen river. The boat was carrying his family and twenty other slaves trying to escape a North Carolina plantation."

Lucius tugged at his vest and straightened his back.

"We don't need to be told about the evils of those who believed in slavery. We must defend our families and homes from the horrors that will be inflicted upon our families if the Ku Klux Klan successfully establishes a den here in Philadelphia!"

Josiah riveted his eyes on Lucius as his thoughts raced back to his and Toby's visit with Honest Abe. An image of a broken wheel replaced that of a toppled wagon, scattered lumber, injured mules, and echoing pistol shots from Waylan Vestry's pistol.

Lucius' eyes moved slowly from man to man. "That's right. You should fear what the Klan will do. If they establish a foothold in our city, no black—man, woman or child—will be safe. Only God knows where the violence will end and who among our friends and families will be the victims."

Lucius pumped his fist and lifted his voice.

"The Invisible Empire's nocturnal armies of men and horses robed in ghostly white will, under the cover of darkness, sweep our city and then on into the North! They'll spread lies and try to turn local and city governments against us.

"Don't you think we're treated harshly now? I tell you that we will soon enter the great tribulation itself! Instead of insults and curses, we'll feel the bloody bite of the lash! Instead of back-alley beatings, we'll find nooses around our necks!"

Josiah stepped forward, his hand gripping the knife at his side. He could not bear the thought of Toby or Angelina falling into the hands of ruthless Klansmen.

"We must stop them!"

Lucius reached out and patted Josiah firmly on the shoulder. He then looked soberly to each man. "We will stop them. We must send the Klan the kind of message they respect and understand. We must show them that we have an army to oppose theirs!"

Billy opened his arms and held out his hands. "There are only five of us! We can't defeat the entire Klan!"

Lucius raised a hand and cut Billy off. "If we strike first and strike hard, I believe we can turn them away from Philadelphia, but only if we strike before they do."

Lucius turned and picked up the lantern. Holding it by the handle, he lifted it to eye level. The bright light clearly illumined every face in the circle.

"The Bible tells us not to hide our light under a bushel and that a city on a hill cannot be hid. Therefore, we'll shine our light from a high hill. Our actions will speak louder than any words in a newspaper or from a pulpit!"

In one swift motion, Lucius reached up and turned down the lantern to a glowing golden ball. He crossed the room and opened the door.

"Follow me!"

The ease with which the five men traveled unseen along the riverfront amazed Josiah. The moon not only gave them enough silvery light to move quickly, it also created innumerable shadows in which to hide. Lucius led them steadily north, block after block, snaking through back alleys and narrow unlit streets behind warehouses and shops.

Only twice did Josiah notice others in the darkness. Once, early on, they avoided two security guards patrolling the docks near an expensive schooner. Then, shortly after, he spied three young whites dangling their legs from a pier and smoking cigars.

Almost an hour later, Lucius raised his hand and stopped his winded band of warriors. Standing at the end of a dark alley, they'd come to the edge of the business district. Two- and three-story buildings gave way to a low horizon of trees, private residences and streetlights.

Billy stepped to Lucius' side. "Enough's enough. You've been leadin' us on nearly an hour. What's your plan?"

Josiah leaned in to hear Lucius' answer, with Horace and Harold looming over his shoulder.

"My plan? Why it's exactly what I told you back at the warehouse." Lucius lifted his arm and pointed to a grass-topped rise three-quarters of a mile away. "We're going to shine our light from a hill."

Deep-voiced Horace shook his head. "I don't get it. We're goin' to burn somethin'?"

Moving around Billy, Josiah's searching eyes found the large, regal house on the crest. An icy tingle shot down Josiah's back as he finally realized what Lucius intended to do. He spun around.

With a low laugh, Lucius shook his head no. "My friend, the Klan burns crosses. Our warnings will be more direct. We'll burn houses."

Three of the four men grew suddenly still, their eyes widening.

Josiah, however, pushed his way in front of Billy.

"How do you know that house belongs to a Klansman? Don't they keep their identities secret?"

Lucius answered calmly. "You're right. But secrets can be found out. For several months our backers have been investigating the associations of a half-dozen men. One of those men got careless, made a mistake. Our backers discovered his name."

Turning to face the crest, Lucius stared up at the house. "And that's where the Klansman lives. According to our backers, he and his family are out of town. It's probably a cover for Klan business."

Lucius stared straight at Josiah. "You're the one who said that something needed to be done. Well, here's your opportunity."

Josiah thoughts ranged back to that night ten years ago in a farmer's barn. If anybody was accidentally inside that house—

Lucius stepped from the alley and into the dimly lit street. Waving his hand, Lucius motioned them forward.

* * *

Twenty minutes later, the five men arrived at the base of a heavily wooded slope. Tall dense trees hid their view of the house on the crest of the hill above them.

For the second time that night, it struck Josiah as odd how easily they moved about Philadelphia unseen. The feeling stirred both positive and negative emotions: excitement, that they could complete Lucius' plan without being seen, and worry, that the Klan could do the same against the Freedom Press or Angelina's boardinghouse.

Standing in dark shadows beneath a mammoth oak tree, Josiah and the other three men watched silently as Lucius dropped to one knee. Straining, he exhaled a quick blast of air and lifted a large flat rock away from the base of the tree. Then he brushed aside loose dirt from the exact spot where the rock had rested.

Josiah moved around to one side for a closer look. To his surprise, Lucius huffed a second time and removed an equally large sheet of slate.

The other three men leaned in. Lucius reached down into a hole. Moments later, the men backed away and formed a half circle.

Lucius placed a tightly bound black bundle on the ground in front of them, then removed ten thick wooden sticks and an unmarked one-gallon tin. He snapped the cord binding the bundle and handed out what appeared to be sheets of black cloth. Each man, including Lucius, received two pieces.

The four men watched as Lucius stood and shook out his own pieces. The larger piece fell open in the shape of a robe, the smaller into a hood.

A hood! A hood with two holes cut for eyes and a thin slit for the mouth. Josiah gasped. The robe and the hood. Now it all made sense.

Lucius turned his head and nodded. "Josiah seems to have figured out what they're for. Tell the others what you think, Josiah?"

"Disguises. Like the Klan wears."

"That's right," Lucius replied as he handed out long strips of cloth to be used as belts. "Our own official uniforms. We're soldiers now, soldiers of the night. Let's get dressed."

Billy chuckled and slipped the robe over his head and shoulders.

Josiah donned his robe and hood.

Looking out the roughly cut holes, he felt as if he had suddenly entered a different world. His view was narrowed due to the shape of the holes. Yet, in another way, his view was broadened. He felt like an entirely different person in a place where man's laws no longer applied.

As he started to tie the strip of black cloth around his waist, he decided against it. Stuffing the strip of cloth into his back pocket, he removed his leather belt from his pants and rebuckled it outside the robe. Now he could reach the knife!

Josiah adjusted the hood and position of the eyeholes, then looked up.

Lucius, robed and hooded, handed each man two sticks and then bent down and opened the gallon tin.

The sight unnerved Josiah. Billy, Horace and Harold had already left. Instead, he saw three black caricatures of men. The only visible human parts were their hands and the whites of their eyes.

Josiah then glanced to the open tin. It was easy to guess what was inside.

"All right, listen up!" Lucius commanded. "Follow my instructions precisely. I'll lead the way up the hill. When we reach the house, Billy, you and I will break left and cover the back and far side. Horace and Harold, you break right and take the near side. Josiah, you'll follow them and then continue on to the front of the house. My signal will be a quick three-part whistle."

Lucius tossed each man a box of matches, then pointed at the tin. "This is pitch. It's hard to extinguish and it burns real hot. When you hear my signal, strike your match and light your torches. Throw them through the windows. One torch for each level, ground and upper. Just like God's judgment in days of old, not a single wall will remain standing. Everybody understand?"

The men nodded and began dipping and stirring their sticks in the thick pitch. In less than a minute, the tip of every stick was coated black.

Lucius stuffed the can back into the hole and repositioned the slate and the rock. Then, with a curt nod, Lucius started up the path between the trees.

Josiah waited until the other men passed and then took the rear. As they climbed the hill, he thought about Lucius' judgment against the Klan. They deserved stern judgment, no question. Burning an empty house did not compare with taking someone's life, and the Klan had certainly taken many lives.

Within minutes, they reached the clearing just below the top of the hill. Swathed in moonlight, the wide, two-story house stood silhouetted against a starry sky.

"And remember our backup plan if anything happens," Lucius said quietly. "We'll meet back at the warehouse."

With a short wave of his arm, Lucius signaled Horace and Harold to the right. Their robes rustling, the two brothers lumbered across the grass, torches in hand.

Billy broke into a run toward the left side of the house. Lucius waved Josiah to the front, then turned and followed Billy.

Josiah hurried across the lawn. Reaching the house, he dropped to one knee in the shadows at the corner of the front porch.

The time for worrying was over. He needed to work fast. He took out a match, then glanced up nervously across the porch at the front windows. The house was completely dark.

A frightened meow near Josiah's feet preceded a bolt of white between his legs.

Startled, Josiah lost his balance and dropped one of the torches. He groped for the lower rail of the porch to steady himself.

His hand missed and instead struck an empty bottle that had been left sitting beside the rail. The bottle shot across the porch, glanced noisily off the front door and bounded down the front steps onto a slate walk.

Josiah cringed as the bottle struck the stone, expecting the bottle to break loudly into a dozen pieces. Instead, it pinged off the stone and plopped quietly into the grass.

Stupid cat!

Josiah picked up the torch he had dropped and forced himself to the task at hand. Lucius still had not whistled. Fortunately, he had not dropped the matches.

The creak of an opening door froze Josiah. He flattened his back to the porch, keeping a rose bush between himself and the door. He heard cautious footsteps only ten feet away!

He slowly turned his head and peeked over his shoulder. He did not need to see the yellow glow of a low-burning lamp inside the house to know somebody was home. How could this be? Lucius said they were all gone!

To Josiah's growing fright, he heard a second set of footsteps on the porch behind him.

What could he do? To reach the woods, he would have to run across a couple hundred feet of open yard in plain view of whoever stood on the porch.

A dull metallic click sharpened Josiah's fright to near terror. The Klansman had cocked a rifle!

Josiah nearly melted into the ground when a deep voice whispered above him.

"Tom. You go around to the right. John, you take the left. I'll cover the front."

Josiah's heart sank. There were three Klansmen, not two! And one of them would pass right by him!

A low, three-part whistle broke the silence.

Seconds later, a loud crackle caused Josiah's head to swing around. The dark edge of the forest to his right flickered with reflected orange firelight.

One of the men above Josiah exclaimed loudly. "Around the side! And to the back!"

The front door banged open, followed by the sound of feet

moving quickly across the porch. A tall, lanky man bounded heavily down the front steps, rifle out in front of him.

Moments later, two shots rang out from around the far side of the house, followed by angry shouting.

Josiah dropped his torches and broke away from the porch towards the woods and the path that led down the hill.

"Hey, Tom! There goes one of them!" a deep voice yelled from behind him.

Glancing to his right, Josiah saw flames shooting out of two upstairs windows. The trees facing the back of the house glowed with orange and yellow light.

And someone was running across the grass directly at him.

Panic coursed through Josiah. The ever-changing position of the hood's eyeholes obstructed his vision. And worse, the Klansman had the angle on him! They'd reach the woods at the same moment!

The distance closed between them.

Twenty feet. Ten feet. Five.

Josiah's hand dropped to his belt. In one swift motion, he pulled the knife from its sheath and lashed sideways.

His pursuer saw the flash of steel a second too late. As he twisted to avoid the knife, the sharp blade slashed deeply across his outstretched arm, just below the elbow. With a loud cry, he tripped and tumbled to the ground, clutching his left arm.

Seconds later, Josiah crashed through heavy underbrush. Bearing to his right, he stumbled onto the trail that wound through the trees to the bottom of the hill.

Breathing raggedly, Josiah bolted recklessly down the rock-strewn path into the safety of the darkness with the knife still clutched in his hand.

15

The knock on Josiah's bedroom door came far too early.

"It's six-thirty. Breakfast in five minutes!" Toby announced cheerfully.

Josiah moaned and rolled over on his back. He rubbed his eyes. Only three hours sleep! Lucky for him, Friday's workload was always light. With this week's *Freedman's Journal* now on the newsstands, Toby would finally relax a little. They would clean the presses, refill supplies and tend to general housekeeping.

He pushed himself upright in the bed.

Sitting, he turned and swung his feet to the floor. As he did, a brief wave of dizziness struck him. Josiah studied his hands. Luckily, he had not stained himself with the pitch.

From the kitchen, a smooth tenor voice singing *Amazing Grace* wafted down the hall and through the closed door.

Josiah breathed deeply and rose from the bed. What would Toby say and do if he ever discovered that his newly promoted apprentice had served as a soldier of the night?

Even though Lucius had been mistaken about the Klansman being home, they had successfully completed their goal. No one had been hurt in the exchange, except Harold, and that was his own doing. Getting away, he had run full speed into a tree at the bottom of the hill and had broken a couple of fingers.

Maybe now the Klan would get the message! Philadelphia would not allow bigotry and violence against blacks.

The smell of frying bacon drifted by Josiah's nose. Now he would have to look Toby straight in the eye and talk and act as if nothing had happened.

Josiah slipped on a pair of pants. Looking in the mirror on the wall by his bed, he noticed puffy wrinkles under his drooping eyes. He frowned.

He tried to rub them away. What he really needed was to splash his face with cold water, but that would now have to wait until after breakfast.

After facing Toby.

Josiah walked into the kitchen and took his regular seat facing the stove. He glanced over his shoulder at the center bookcase. He had put Daniel's knife back in its place on top of the old Bible. Carefully cleaned, the knife and its sheath held no evidence of the night's bloody skirmish with the Klan.

Hearing the scrape of Josiah's chair, Toby looked back over his shoulder as he stirred a batch of scrambled eggs.

"Morning. Sleep well?"

The pleasant tone of Toby's voice helped relieve Josiah's growing tension. He returned a weak smile. "Not real well, but enough to get through a day's work."

Josiah looked down the hall. He noticed that the door to Sam's room was open. "Where's Daniel?"

"On his way to the station. He's taking the early train to Washington." Turning around from the stove, Toby served their plates. "Coffee?"

Josiah nodded through an unexpected yawn.

Toby poured two steaming mugs and sat down. "I didn't sleep all that well myself. Woke up once near midnight and then again at four. Never went back to sleep. Your turn to bless the meal."

Josiah lowered his eyes and folded his hands in his lap. Guilt stabbed at his conscience. He searched for something meaningful to say.

"Lord, thank you for watching over Sam, Toby, Angelina and me. Deliver us from evil and let the wicked harvest their just rewards."

Toby shot Josiah a puzzled glance, adding, "and give us this day our daily bread. Forgive us our transgressions, Lord, which are too many to count. Amen."

Josiah avoided Toby's eyes and reached for his mug of coffee.

Ten minutes later, as the two men cleared the table, Toby explained his plan for the morning.

"We've got a new job to print by ten. Then you need to deliver that order for Reverend Thompson. Remember, they live north of town on the same property as the church we attend. You can use Angelina's horse and buggy. How's that sound?"

Toby's directions proved unnecessary, but Josiah could not tell him that. His midnight escapade had taken him along the edge of several spacious properties, one of which had been the church.

Josiah snapped the reins lightly and Angelina's filly picked up her pace. Thoughts of seeing Christine made the morning's work race by: finishing the print run, getting the buggy from the livery, and loading the boxes of flyers and letterhead.

Turning his head toward the small rise three-quarters of a mile away, Josiah watched a faint column of smoke drift over the trees. As he suspected, the house on the hill still smoldered. Two tall blackened chimneys stood alone on the charred hilltop, the only remains of the Klansman's home.

The sight flooded Josiah with unexpected emotions. As much as he hated the Klan, he hoped that no one had died in the blaze.

A quarter mile farther, Josiah turned onto a shady, tree-lined lane leading to the church and Reverend Thompson's house. A hundred yards down, the lane broke clear of the trees and split into two directions. To the left, the lane wound around a grassy slope back into the woods toward the church. Josiah could see the steeple peaking up out of the top of the trees not far away. Above the steeple, dark wisps from the Klansman's smoking rubble stained the blue sky.

He followed the lane to the right around a sharp bend bordered by the woods, suddenly finding himself near the front gate to Reverend Thompson's yard. A white picket fence bordered the simple, but tidy two-story farmhouse.

Christine stood behind the gate, her hands stuffed into the pockets of her coveralls. Underneath, she wore an old cotton blouse with the sleeves rolled up to her elbows; and with her hair twisted into a thick braid, she looked like quite a different girl from the one he had met at church or at the Freedom Press.

Anxious, Josiah brought the buggy to a halt and jumped down. How could she have been expecting him?

Christine opened the gate and stepped through, her serious expression softening.

"Hi. I thought I just might see you out here this morning."

Josiah hesitated as he came around the buggy. He tried to keep his head from turning to the left toward the smoke drifting over the treetops. He stammered out his question. "You thought you'd see me? Why's that?"

Christine glanced up at the smoke, then back to Josiah. "Toby told my father he'd deliver the last batch of printing. With Sam out of town and Toby in charge of the shop, I figured he would send you."

Reaching for the first box, Josiah spoke over his shoulder. "Where does your father want them?"

"We're taking them to the church," she replied as she climbed into the buggy.

"Makes sense." Josiah pushed the box back into its place, then pulled himself up onto the seat.

He picked up the reins and whistled. The buggy jerked forward and started back down the lane toward the church and the rising column of smoke.

At the fork, Christine had Josiah turn down a heavily rutted lane that led through thick woods to the church. He glanced at Christine and her coveralls. "Looks like you're dressed for a good bit of dirty work."

She nodded as a sad expression stole over her face. "Mr. Buck's house was burned down. By God's grace they survived, even though they lost everything. I'm sure you saw the smoke on your way here. I'm going to help clear the site later this afternoon."

Nodding, Josiah took a long, deep breath. She had not mentioned anything about an attack by five cloaked men.

"Do you know what happened?" he asked tentatively.

"Not exactly. I think Father said it was an accident. He didn't say how."

Josiah looked down at his feet and for the first time he noticed that the toe of his right boot was splattered with pitch. Fear shot through him. How could it have happened? Then he remembered the moment when the cat surprised him and he had dropped the torch. It must have bumped against his boot!

What if Christine noticed?

Josiah fought down rising fear as the buggy rumbled out from under the trees into a wide clearing. Off to the right on a flat rectangle of ground, the church sat with its back to a steep hill. Tall, narrow and white, the church was backdropped by the spring green of the grassy field and tree line.

Parked to the left of the front steps were two empty wagons. A saddled horse nibbled at the grass nearby. Josiah felt his throat tighten. Something was up and it wasn't hard to guess what!

Christine sat forward on the seat as Josiah slowed the buggy. "I suspect that Father's offered Jason Buck and his family use of the cottage up on the hill." She pointed.

Josiah followed her finger. Though he had attended the church twice with Sam, Toby and Angelina, he had never noticed the cottage.

"I also suspect they won't be needing it too long," Christine continued. "Jason Buck's a well-respected man. I'm sure the congregation will help him out."

Jumping from the buggy, Josiah walked slowly around to the other side. He tried to sort out the conflict between Lucius' information about the Klansman and what Christine had just said. But that's what the Klan was all about, wasn't it? Men who acted one way in public but another when night fell.

Christine stood waiting with her back to the church.

A sober voice called from behind her.

"Daughter. Josiah." Reverend Thompson descended the

steps of the church. Concern lined his face. His eyes were bloodshot. Obviously, he had lost a lot of sleep. "Thank you for bringing the rest of my order."

"Yes, sir." Josiah pulled a box from the back of the buggy. "Where would you like me to put these?"

"Please put them on the shelves in the storage closet past the foyer."

"I'll help Josiah," Christine said cheerfully. She turned around sharply and collided into Josiah, whose sight had been obstructed by the box on his shoulder.

"Sorry!" she exclaimed, pausing briefly to rub her ankle where his boot had struck hers.

Grabbing the box with his free hand, Josiah steadied his load and continued up the steps. One trip later, all the boxes were inside. For several minutes, he helped Christine empty the boxes onto the shelves. On his way toward the front door, Josiah stopped suddenly, his shoulders stiffening. He stepped back.

A tall, lanky man stood sideways on the front steps. A younger man sat facing him. Both men had curly coal black hair and fair skin. A wagon was now parked beside Angelina's buggy. What seized Josiah's attention, however, was the bloodstained dressing wrapped tightly around the young man's left forearm.

Then Josiah recognized who they were. They were two of the men whose house had been torched, including the one he had slashed with Daniel's knife!

Christine stared at the dressing. She walked around Josiah and onto the steps. "Mr. Buck, what happened to Tom?"

Josiah hung back. Now, in the daylight, this man and his son did not seem much like Klansmen. Still, looks could be deceiving.

Jason glanced pensively at his son's arm, then back to Christine. He did not seem to notice Josiah standing in the shadows of the foyer. "We were attacked by three or four men decked out in black hoods and robes. One of them slit Tom's forearm open with a knife. He's fortunate that I've dressed a hundred wounds like his before—one of the few good things I learned from the War. He'll have no strength in his arm for a week or so, but it'll heal. He's a tough kid.

"What's more serious is the fact those hoodlums escaped." Jason lowered his voice. "They're a vicious lot, torching a house at that time of the morning. Lucky we were still up. Since the Missis died, my boys and I keep odd hours. Still, there was nothing we could do to stop the flames. The house was burning on three sides, top and bottom, at the same time. A Klan tactic for sure. Takes a building, house or barn right down to the ground."

Startled by the touch of Reverend Thompson's hand on his shoulder, Josiah jumped back.

"Sorry, son. Didn't mean to surprise you."

The reverend stepped outside with a small sack in his hand. "We don't have any proof the Klan's involved. I know there's certain rumors around and about, but jumping to conclusions will only worsen matters."

At last, Jason noticed Josiah. "I wasn't saying that the Klan was responsible, but that their methods had been used. Reverend, I told you earlier that I thought the men who burned my house down were all blacks. No offense intended to the young man here."

For a second, all eyes turned toward Josiah. His heart pounded. He hoped the fear rising inside him would not show on his face.

Reverend Thompson stepped in front of Josiah and walked down the steps toward the wagon, drawing everyone's worried gazes away.

Except Christine's.

The reverend shook his head and set the sack in the wagon. "That doesn't make any sense. Nobody around here questions your commitment to freedmen and their issues. Without your leadership in the Underground Railroad, hundreds of blacks would have never escaped the South. And your valor serving the Union in the War is equally well-known."

Jason squinted his red-lined eyes. "We'll see. I promised I'd keep a lid on this thing and I will. The last thing we need is a public uproar. And thanks for the use of the cottage. We'll be at the old homestead most of the day clearing it out."

The former Union soldier and his son climbed into their wagon. With a flip of the reins, the twin horses jerked the wagon into motion.

Solemnly, Josiah descended the steps and trudged his way to the buggy. He pulled himself up onto the seat and took the reins.

The feel of Christine's eyes on his back caused him to glance over his shoulder. For a brief second, their eyes met and locked. Christine hesitantly waved goodbye.

Josiah waved back, then turned around and whistled sharply. Angelina's horse snorted once, then began the journey home down the rutted lane.

16

To Adam's surprise, the second floor of the Public Ledger Building was empty. He crossed the hall and approached his father's office. Quietly, he cracked the door ajar.

He heard his father cough. Then he heard the repeated crinkling of paper. Maybe he was folding the map!

Adam was tempted to burst in, but an angry string of curses from his father stopped him with his hand on the doorknob. Adam glanced both ways down the long hall. Still empty!

His attention snapped back to the crack in the door. The crinkling of paper ceased suddenly, followed by a loud click, two brief metallic squeaks and a second click.

Adam could not hold back any longer. He edged the door closed, knocked loudly, then casually opened the door and poked his head and arm into the room with a cheerful expression and a wave just like he often did.

Waylan, standing by his desk, lifted a cigar to his mouth. "Well, haven't seen much of you lately. Come on in. How's Ed Biggs treating our brightest apprentice compositor these days?"

"He treats me well," Adam answered as he stepped into the room. He studied his father's placid face. If he was hiding something, he surely was not showing it. Not that that meant anything; his father had always been a good poker player. He had bluffed many a man into playing out a losing hand.

Waylan struck a match and lit his cigar. A thin cloud of gray smoke quickly formed above his head. "Good. Just like your old man. Start at the bottom; work hard and work up. Sooner or later you'll find yourself somewhere near the top. Then it'll be up to you to make the most of your opportunity. You can't let anyone or anything stand in your way. That's the long and short of it. And if that's the only thing I ever teach you, it's enough to get you through life and get you what you want."

Waylan sat down in his chair. It creaked as he leaned forward to study a report lying open in the middle of his desk. "Now if you don't mind, I've got to get back to business. Keep up the good work. I'll speak with Ed later this afternoon and find out what new opportunities he's planning for you this summer."

Adam nodded silently, turned and left the room. He slowly closed the door. After looking both ways down the hall, he paused and put his ear near the door.

The creak of the chair preceded approaching footsteps. Adam started quickly down the hall until he heard his father throwing the lock from the inside. He stepped closer and heard a click, followed by two brief metallic squeaks and a second click.

He shook his head. What was that sound? Sooner or later he would figure it out!

Adam turned and headed for the stairs to the third floor.

While Christine helped her father and the Buck family clear the rubble from their fire-blackened homesite, Josiah and Toby began a print job for the Pennsylvania Freedman's Relief Association. The hard, fast-paced work helped Josiah focus his thoughts and ignore the worry that had been knotting in his stomach all afternoon.

Meeting Jason Buck and his son at the church had just been the beginning. The ache only increased after his prearranged meeting with Lucius at the Market Street Printing Supply on his way back to the Freedom Press.

"Tonight. The warehouse. At midnight," Lucius had explained, angling his hat low over his eyes. "Everybody's coming, even Harold with his busted fingers. We're going to strike again, while the iron's hot. We'll really get the Klan's attention tonight."

Josiah had listened and stared at his feet as his stomach twisted painfully. He could not bring himself to tell Lucius that he had met the Klansmen who had owned the house on the hill. Maybe it was the fierce, bitter look in Lucius' eyes. Or maybe it was the fact that he could not reconcile what Christine had told him and what he had heard for himself in the conversation between Jason Buck and Pastor Thompson.

It was all so confusing. That's what made the Klan so dangerous. Men who smile and call you by name during the day could curse and hang you come night!

Josiah looked up from the printing press to find Toby staring straight at him.

"Son, you all right?"

"I guess so." Josiah knew he needed more information. "Is it true that the Klan's trying to work its way into Philadelphia?"

Toby's eyes narrowed sharply. "Where'd you hear that rumor?"

The lie formed quickly. "In the alley outside the printing supply shop from two wagoners. They were upset, like it wasn't rumor, but fact."

Toby sighed. His shoulders sagged as he rubbed his hand along his brow. "It's time we had a talk. Let's go upstairs."

"That's one of the reasons why Sam and Angelina are in Washington. They're trying to convince a special commission that the Klan is trying to move North and that Philadelphia is one of their first targets. Those hellions couldn't have picked a more dangerous time, here on the eve of the ten-year anniversary of Lincoln's Emancipation Proclamation."

Toby folded his large hands in front of him on the table. The creases around his eyes deepened. "Sam's got the mayor believing him, and Senator Scott of Pennsylvania, too. He wants the Senate to open an immediate investigation and put an end to what the Klan's planning before it gets any worse. First, they burn down a warehouse and nearly start a riot. Then, they sabotage Honest Abe's wagons and try to run him out of business. Now, with the fire at Jason Bucks, where will it all end?"

Josiah nodded, pride suddenly swelling up inside. If only Toby knew what he and Lucius and the others were doing without the help of Washington! By the time the government decided to do something, they'd have already run the Klan out of the state!

"Where will it end?" Toby repeated softly, his eyes moving from his hands to Josiah's face. "We fought a long, bloody war to stop this kind of evil, but Sam was right. Shedding each other's blood couldn't heal the bitterness or hatred, North or South, white or black. The Klan feeds on the evil in men's hearts, stirrin' up anger and violence. They think themselves chivalrous and call themselves patriots, but they're really nothin' more than two-faced liars and murderers like their father the Devil."

Toby's jaw and neck muscles tightened. His hands opened and closed, like two huge black vises. Josiah had never seen such a hurt expression on Toby's face. His eyes were open wide, staring into space, fixed on some memory Josiah couldn't see.

Without warning, he slapped the table so hard Josiah nearly sprang out of his seat.

In one motion, Toby pushed himself out of his chair and away from the table. With his arms extended, he leaned against the kitchen counter by the potbellied stove. "I'll feel much better when Sam, Angelina and Daniel get back safely Monday night."

Josiah slid out of his chair and walked around the table, not knowing what to say or do.

Toby took a deep breath. "After you clean the presses, use the rest of the afternoon to better yourself, do a little reading, or the like."

"Yes, sir." Josiah backed away.

Without looking up, Toby nodded.

Josiah made himself busy. Using a cleaning compound that made him dizzy if he smelled too much of it, he worked each press in turn until there was not a dab of leftover ink anywhere. Two hours later, after cleaning his hands and arms, Josiah retreated down the hall, entered his room, and closed the door behind him.

He stepped to the window overlooking busy Chestnut Street, drawn by the clippity-clop of hoofs and the rumble of wooden wheels over cobblestone. Three of Honest Abe's freight cars loaded down with sealed barrels rolled by, the drivers obviously taking it slow. Two horsemen accompanied the cars, one at the front and one at the back. Honest Abe was not taking any chances with whatever valuable commodity the wagons were carrying.

Turning his head, Josiah glanced over at his desk in the corner. On it lay the journal and pen Toby had given him as gifts. He saw Daniel's gift, too, his book about his life on the Cherokee Trail of Tears.

Josiah glanced at his pocket watch. It was a long time until midnight. If last night's lesson taught him nothing else, he knew he needed to be alert and ready for anything.

He plopped onto his bed and closed his eyes. At the edge of his thoughts, familiar but faint voices whispered warnings. Toby cleaning the cut above his eye, telling him to let it go; Angelina at the train station, talking about invisible battles and century wars and the Devil; Daniel at the dinner table, echoing the words Toby had written in his note, how God brings secret things into judgment.

For few seconds, he listened to the voices but could not figure out why they suddenly came to mind. Somehow, he sensed it was all very important. But what did it all mean? Maybe, if he had written everything down as Toby had suggested . . . .

But weariness stole over him as surely as the night and the caring voices faded to silence.

In moments he was sound asleep.

17

His afternoon nap and a dinner of boiled potatoes, chunks of beef and leftover vegetables had energized Josiah. And with Toby turning in early, getting out of the house had been even easier than on the night before.

As he hurried down the shadow-draped alley, the sounds of his boots echoed softly between the buildings. Josiah gripped the handle of Daniel Sweetwater's knife hanging from his belt.

The problems of Daniel's generation had not changed all that much in thirty years. Bigoted, hateful men still sought to rule over everyone else. It was still a white man's world.

As he rounded the corner at the back of the deserted warehouse, he glanced out over the docks at the Delaware River. Stopping at the door at the end of the pier's weathered boardwalk, Josiah quietly knocked three times in quick succession. A second later, the door opened silently.

A thin bar of amber light slanted across the boardwalk at Josiah's feet. He pushed the door open just enough to slip inside.

He was met by a serious-faced Lucius and a firm pat on the shoulder. "Good. Everyone's here."

Unlike at their first meeting, no one asked questions or made small talk. The expressions on everyone's faces were different, sober.

Lucius opened a crate in the back corner and handed out the black robes and hoods.

"Our backers have identified another Klansman. The enemy has infiltrated our city and our community's most trusted institutions. We must be strong and courageous if we want to defeat the Klan."

Josiah started to unfold his robe.

Lucius nodded. "Josiah's on the right track. We'll put on the robes before we leave tonight," he commanded, stepping to the center of the room and turning down the lantern.

"The Klan will be more on guard. We can't afford to be recognized.

"Now, slip on your hoods and robes, and let's get moving!"

The route through Philadelphia's north side was the same one they had taken the night before. Forty-five minutes after leaving the warehouse, the city gave way to farmland and scattered farmhouses. Confident from their previous night's trek, the black-robed band moved invisibly from homestead to homestead beneath a cloud-darkened sky.

Josiah glanced to his left. Jason Buck's rubble-covered hilltop was less than a half-mile away. Lucius stepped out from behind a tree and waved the group forward across an intersection. One of the roads wound up a small slope into the pine forest directly across from where they had exited the grove of apple trees.

One by one, they bolted across the open space. Josiah brought up the rear.

As he crossed to the far side of the intersection and joined the others in the shadows beneath the pines, Josiah suddenly realized where they were.

The sickening knot in his stomach abruptly returned.

He spun and studied the road, hoping he was wrong. But he was not. The apple grove, the tall pines, the three-way intersection and a road winding up a slope into the woods confirmed that they now stood at the main entrance to the church. And just a hundred yards or so away, down a rutted lane through the woods, stood Christine Thompson's home! Certainly Lucius wouldn't bring them here!

"Josiah!" Lucius called softly. "C'mon!"

The black-robed band moved quickly up the dirt road. Less

than a minute later, they stopped at the edge of the pines facing a large grassy field. Across the field stood the Methodist church, its tall white steeple reaching toward the clouds scattered across the sky.

Near a large outcropping of rock just inside the woods, Lucius had Billy pull away a large flat stone and uncover another hidden cache of torches and pitch.

Josiah felt nauseous as he watched Lucius. Maybe they were just passing through the church property to another farmhouse.

Lucius handed each man foot-long torches. Everyone dipped them into the pitch. Josiah was the last. As he lowered his torch into the thick, inky liquid, he felt as though his hands were not his own.

Lucius tossed each man a box of matches.

"I've been told that the church is always left open. Between the four of you, you have eight torches. From my signal, I want you in and out in less than a minute. Main sanctuary and upper balcony. Once it gets burning, nobody can stop it."

Horrified, Josiah glanced at Billy, then at Harold and Horace. None of them seemed to care that they were going to burn down a church! If fact, they were excited!

Lucius kept four torches for himself. He lifted one and pointed to the right across the field at an opening in the woods some fifty yards away.

"Down that narrow road is the Klansman's house. In his side yard are several tall bales of hay. Your signal is firelight shining over the trees. Then hit the church. We'll meet back in the apple grove at the intersection behind us."

Josiah's throat constricted as pain lanced through his stomach. Why would Lucius set fire to Reverend Thompson and Christine's house? They weren't associated with the Klan! They were good people!

Josiah shuddered. The four pairs of eyes staring out from behind the roughly cut holes no longer seemed human. They were filled with malicious intent toward a man, his daughter and a church about which they knew nothing.

With a brisk wave of his arm, Lucius motioned them into action. As they crossed the field to the church, Josiah watched Lucius angle farther and farther away from their group, then finally disappear into the woods.

They climbed the steps to the church, torches unlit but in hand. Billy tested the door. Lucius was right. The door was unlocked.

After adjusting his black robe and hood, Josiah turned on the top step and stared out over the trees in the direction of the house. The ache in his stomach sharpened into a cramp, and the torches he carried felt as heavy as iron.

He pictured Reverend Thompson's and Christine's smiling faces. He remembered snatches of conversations they'd had, the kindness they'd shown him and their genuine concern. How could the reverend possibly have any partnership with the Klan?

The answer came from deep within his heart.

Dropping the torches, Josiah leapt down the steps and started up the dirt road toward the house.

"Hey! Where you goin'?" Billy called.

Josiah ignored him and broke into a run. His thoughts were far ahead of his pumping legs as he raced up the rutted road and into the dark mouth of the woods.

Tall pines closed in around him as the moon momentarily broke through the clouds, casting its silver light through the treetops above him. His eyes were trained straight ahead, hoping against hope that he would not see a burst of bright firelight. He had no way to know how far Lucius was ahead of him. And even if he caught up with Lucius, what could he do? Lucius was bigger and stronger and more determined to complete his acts of violence.

Violence. The thought of seeing Christine or her father hurt struck panic into him as he broke free of the woods and started up the curved, grassy rise toward the house.

Then, through the eyeholes of his hood, he saw tongues of red and yellow light flare up behind the rise.

"No!" Josiah screamed raggedly, his voice breaking through the constriction in his throat.

He stumbled at the top of the lane a hundred feet from the farmhouse. From his knees, he watched long tendrils of flame lick up the right side of the house from an open window, crackling furiously and reaching to the roof.

Lucius was nowhere to be seen. Josiah climbed to his feet and ran toward the front gate, then ducked behind a large oak tree just outside the fence.

The reverend and his daughter, wearing only their nightclothes, staggered barefoot out the front door, coughing and holding their hands over their mouths and noses. Christine's father motioned her out into the yard. Then he turned and staggered back through the door into the house.

Over the growing roar of the spreading fire, Josiah could hear Christine as she ran back to her father.

"No!" she cried, clutching at his arm. "You can't go back inside!"

Her father yanked his arm free of her grasp and reentered the house. Christine pleaded hysterically through the open door, her arms outstretched, her body shaking.

Then, to Josiah's shock, she darted in after her father. Josiah stepped away from the tree and pushed open the gate. Why would she dare go back inside? The fire was out of control and covered the entire roof!

Making his decision instantly, Josiah sprinted up the walk to the porch. The heat penetrated his robe and hood.

He stopped at the open door and poked his head inside. Smoke filled the house, but more frightening than the smoke was the noise. Josiah had never heard such a thunderous roar! The old, dried timber, with a high ceiling and open windows on every side, gave the hungry fire free roam of the house.

A sharp crash above Josiah's head jerked his eyes upward. Had parts of the roof caved in?

Slow-moving shapes appeared unexpectedly in the smoke: Christine and her father!

Josiah stepped into the living room. Thick, billowing gray smoke instantly stung his eyes. The ceiling groaned above him as he ripped off his hood and stuffed it into his belt.

He heard Christine's voice. Her cries sounded faint even though she was less than ten feet away! Her father had collapsed to his knees. Spilled across the floor in front of him was an empty box and dozens of photographs and daguerreotypes. Christine pulled at his arm, but her father did not respond.

The smoke!

A second crash snapped his eyes back up to the ceiling just in time to see a huge, burning beam break through and crash into the living area with an explosive spew of sparks and orange flame.

A foot-long piece of timber bounced and struck the reverend on the shoulder, sprawling him to the floor. Christine shrieked and fell back against the wall.

The whole ceiling creaked, then sank nearly two feet in the middle. Debris and furniture from the second floor tumbled through the fire-filled opening into the living area in a furnace of flame and heat.

Weeping and coughing, Christine grabbed her father by the arms and tried to drag him across the floor.

Too slow! Josiah's thoughts screamed. The ceiling's ready to collapse!

He charged into the smoke.

At the sudden sight of black-robed Josiah by her side, Christine nearly stumbled backwards into the fire that crept up the wall behind her.

Josiah grabbed her arm just in time.

Their eyes met briefly. Josiah saw her disbelief, then sudden anger. He had no time for explanations.

Slipping their arms under her father's, together they dragged him across the floor and out onto the porch.

"Farther!" Josiah shouted. Though almost at the point of collapsing herself, Christine obeyed.

They pulled him down the steps and across the grass.

"Beyond the fence!" Josiah commanded as Christine started to let go. Clenching her teeth, Christine sucked in a ragged breath and coughed.

Thirty agonizing seconds later, they were beyond the gate at a grassy patch beneath the tall oak tree. As they lowered her father to the ground, the front of the house collapsed inward, launching a huge mushroom of smoke, fire and sparks upwards into the dark sky.

Even from their position just outside the fence, a searing wave of heat nearly scorched their faces, forcing them to quickly pull her father even farther out into the road.

Josiah stood up. Christine sat barefooted in her nightclothes by her father, his head in her lap. Her long hair was tangled and sweaty, her face marked with despair. She looked up, her eyes consuming Josiah from head to toe.

He stepped back, keenly aware of how terrible and how condemning his black robe surely appeared. Once again, his stomach cramped and his throat constricted. What could he say!

Wild, bright flames engulfed the old farmhouse behind Christine, illuminating the entire yard all the way to the lane and edge of the woods. By morning, there would be nothing but ashes and charred stone.

Tears spilled down her cheeks as she looked off in the distance.

Josiah turned. Beyond the woods, the glow of an even larger fire appeared. The church building was being destroyed, too.

"Go, Josiah," Christine commanded softly. "Go before someone comes and finds you."

Unable to respond, Josiah hesitated briefly, then turned and broke into a full run.

At the edge of the woods, Josiah turned and looked back at the raging fire. Christine, sitting at the top of the rise, lifted her father's head and slid out from under him. Her face racked with pain, she pushed herself to her feet, then hobbled a few feet down the road.

She bent over and picked up a large piece of sewn black cloth.

His hood!

18

Staring out of his second floor window in the Public Ledger Building, Waylan Vestry clasped his hands behind his back. His dark brown eyes drifted absentmindedly from a passing streetcar below to the Liberty Bell atop the State House. His lips curled upward as he considered his swiftly unfolding plan.

Lucius and his recruits successfully burned down the Methodist church and rectory. Reverend Thompson and Jason Buck could no longer refuse the *Public Ledger's* request to print an honest, straightforward account of their tragedies.

Meanwhile, the city's other daily tabloids would be running their own speculative stories—stories that he, Waylan, had planted—about the attacks that would stir fresh hatred between whites and blacks. And after two more attacks by an unsuspecting Lucius and his little band, that hatred would erupt into violence from both sides. Then it would be time for the devastating finale. Not only would Philadelphia turn against freedmen's rights, but so would the entire North as well!

Vestry licked his lips and rocked happily on his heels. His new title as Grand Cyclops and his first den meeting were only three days away. A dozen men were ready to join. When Jennings and Crawford returned Monday morning, they would be pleased by what he had accomplished during their stopover in New York.

His own Klan den! The idea was more intoxicating than any liquor he'd ever drunk!

Vestry turned from the window to his desk and the large map spread out over its surface. He studied the bright red circles drawn over designated locations in and around Philadelphia.

Grand Cyclops! The title and the power would soon be his, and no one was going to stop him!

Toby lifted his foot from the treadle and stopped the press. Josiah, standing at the second press, stared aimlessly out the shop's front window. His foot rested on the treadle, his hand on the platen lever. Toby sighed. The stack of circus posters on the table beside Josiah was a quarter the size of his own stack.

"Son, there's nothing we can do. We're just going to have to wait. Reverend Thompson's life is in the Lord's hands. Jason Buck said he'd swallowed enough smoke to kill two men."

Josiah lowered his eyes to the press and nodded.

"By God's grace, Christine's unhurt," Toby continued in a quiet tone of voice. "We can be thankful for that."

Silently, Josiah nodded a second time.

"You don't look well this morning, but to be honest, I don't feel much like working either," Toby said as he slowly pulled a poster off the press. "We can finish later. Let's go track down Christine. Maybe now she'll tell us what really happened. She and Jason Buck are holding something back. I'm sure of it."

"Yes, sir," was all that Josiah could muster before heading upstairs.

After closing the door to his room, Josiah plopped heavily onto the end of the bed. Resting his elbows on his knees, he buried his face into his hands.

Not only was his career with the Freedom Press soon to be over, but his friendship with Toby and Sam and Angelina, too! Even worse, he could stand trial for burning down the church and house and for the murder of Christine's father if he died!

The weight of his errors pressed down on his shoulders. Throwing the black robe in the river as he ran home in the darkness did little to unload the guilt weighing on his conscience. Christine still had his hood as evidence.

Lifting his head, Josiah glanced around the room. Seeing

Beneath the Sky of an Angry God lying in the middle of the desk reminded him of his dinner with Daniel Sweetwater. What had Daniel said? That if we weren't careful, we could fall to the same temptation and become like those we hate?

But whom could you believe?

Lucius said one thing; Toby and Daniel said another. Worse, he was blocked on every side by people who did not want freedmen to succeed.

Josiah reached under the bed and slid open the trundle drawers. He had to leave Philadelphia, now. What other alternative did he have? He scooped up his clothes and lifted them onto the bed.

As he did, the door opened behind him.

His hands trembling, Josiah slowly turned around. Toby spoke from the hall. "Christine Thompson's here to see you, Josiah. She's waiting in the kitchen."

Josiah hesitated. What could he do? He pushed off the bed and followed Toby into the kitchen. Dread pursued him all the way down the hall.

"I'll leave you two alone," Toby said, heading downstairs into the production room.

Christine sat at the table. Her blue-green eyes flashed with hints of the storm that Josiah knew was within her. Her hair hung down gracefully beneath a rolling rim hat with feathers. She wore a simple blouse and ruffled skirt that were obviously not her proper size, but most likely gifts from a neighbor. Her hands clutched a small purse.

"I told Toby the good news," she explained while keeping her eyes on Josiah. "The doctor says my father's going to pull through."

Josiah sat down across the table from her, swallowed hard and tried to speak, but the words would not come.

Christine opened her handbag. She reached inside and pulled out a bunched-up piece of black cloth and tossed it onto the table.

Josiah looked at the cloth, his eyes wide with horror. His hood! All of Josiah's strength drained out of him. He groaned and slumped down into his chair.

Christine's eyes bored into his, unrelenting.

Josiah wanted to look away but could not.

"You must tell me the truth," Christine demanded. "You know who's responsible for the fires. And right now, I care more about stopping this senseless violence than sparing you. I should've told someone when I first noticed the pitch on your boot. I didn't say anything because the pitch was not actual proof you were involved. But word of what's happened is spreading and tempers are rising fast. We must take action soon. If we don't, more people are going to be hurt. Freedmen will receive the brunt of the retaliation. Tell me it's not true."

Christine's upper lip trembled. "It's up to you, Josiah. Either we go down and talk to Toby, or I'll report what I know."

She picked up the hood and stuffed it back into her handbag without lifting her eyes from his.

Then, to Josiah's surprise, her eyes, which moments earlier blazed angrily, now pleaded earnestly, begging him to make the right decision.

Unsure of the consequences that might follow, he lowered his eyes and nodded.

"Lord Almighty, have mercy!"

Toby's legs gave way and he sat back onto a stool by the front counter. He ran his hands across the top of his hair and turned his head toward the window and street. His eyes teared instantly.

Josiah's stomach cramped, but he did not flinch. Toby's next words caught him completely off guard.

"Son, you're being used," he said soberly. He pulled a handkerchief from his back pocket and wiped his face.

"You and Lucius and the others. There's no more honest, color-blind men in Philadelphia than Jason Buck or Reverend Thompson. How they could be suspected of being Klansmen I can't rightly imagine. For almost twenty years, they've come to the aid of slave and freedmen alike. Jason Buck organized and ran the Underground Railroad before the war."

Toby looked back at Josiah. His voice was pained.

"Evil's afoot once again. I've seen it before, when good men get fooled into doin' the wrong thing, even to the point of killin'."

Christine nodded. "Toby's right, Josiah. Someone's stirring up trouble—ugly, dangerous trouble. We're only four days away from the ten-year celebration of the Emancipation Proclamation."

Josiah watched as Toby's eyes suddenly filled with revelation at Christine's words. He grabbed Josiah's shoulders.

"Son, you've got a lot to answer for. There's no backin' down from your mistakes. But right now, what matters is that you're the only link to the men who give Lucius his instructions."

Toby's eyes were pleading. "Let God turn what the Devil intended for evil into good! Face your mistakes head on and do what's right!"

Squeezing Josiah's shoulders even tighter, Toby asked softly, "So? What are you going to do?"

As Toby let go, Josiah glanced at Christine. The harshness had all but disappeared. Their eyes met.

Did he see forgiveness?

He looked at Toby. The hope in his eyes melted the fear and the shame balled up inside Josiah.

"I'm so sorry," Josiah answered through a deep sigh, his eyes brimming with tears. "I'll do whatever you want me to do."

Relief spread across Toby's and Christine's anxious faces.

Then Toby jumped to his feet.

"I'll get Angelina's buggy. Then we'll go and wire Sam in Washington. That Senate subcommittee needs to know what's going on. Afterwards, we'll drop Christine at her neighbor's house so she can stay with her father. We've no time to waste."

Closing and locking the door to his father's office behind him, Adam turned and faced the room. He brushed his thick brown hair back off his forehead. Several thorough searches of his father's study and bedroom back home had not yielded the elusive map. The map had to be here somewhere.

His eyes moved slowly around the long room. To the left was a barren coat tree, then halfway down the long wall stood his father's open roll-top desk and two-shelf bookcase filled with awards, keepsakes and photographs. A low table sat beneath the windows overlooking Sixth Street and the State House. To his right, matching side chairs sat on either side of a standing suit of medieval armor.

His earlier searches had been fruitless. Adam pounded his fist in his palm.

Blast it! Where did his father keep that map? Surely the map was the key to his father's odd comings and goings and the link between the two Southerners and a shifty freedman!

Quickly crossing the room, Adam searched the desk drawers again. After several frustrating moments, he swiveled around and folded his arms angrily across his chest.

Think! Where could his father hide something he didn't want anyone to stumble across and find? Someplace he could get to quickly and put the map away?

Adam thought back to the time he came in on his father. Right before he opened the door, he heard the crinkle of thick paper followed by a couple of heavy footsteps. Had his father crossed the room toward the desk or away from it?

Glancing back and forth across the office, Adam tried to recall what happened next. As he did, a warm rush started up the back of his neck and raced over the top of his head.

He cocked his head sideways and slowly approached the suit of armor. Now he remembered! He had heard a loud click followed by metallic squeaks.

Metallic squeaks. Of course!

Adam softly thumped the chest of the armor that his father was so fussy about people touching.

A hollow ring! Why hadn't he thought of this before?

He reached up to the helmet and slowly lifted the visor. The metal clicked and then squeaked open.

The corners of Adam's grin edged up into a knowing smile. He carefully stuck his hand into the wide opening where a warrior's face had once been and then reached down.

His fingers brushed a tightly rolled paper cylinder.

19

Clasping his hands behind his back and seething with anger, Waylan Vestry stared out of his office window. He listened silently as Lucius finished his account.

"So, when I returned to the church, Billy and the others were just standing there, torches in hand. Josiah's running off confused them, but I pushed them into action. You know the rest."

After a few more moments of silence, Vestry spoke at last. "And Josiah?"

"Yes, sir. I was just getting to that. On my way to the Freedom Press, I saw Josiah climb into a carriage with the man who runs the print shop and the reverend's daughter."

Vestry spun around, eyes glaring.

Lucius nodded. "And that's not all. When I saw them, they were leaving the telegraph office."

His back stiffening, Vestry closed his hands into fists. "Where did they go after that?"

"I followed them out to a farmhouse not far from the church. A neighbor's, I suppose. They went inside with the reverend's daughter for a few minutes, then returned to the print shop alone. I have a hunch they're keeping Josiah's story among themselves to save his skin."

"They're not keeping it to themselves, you fool! They telegraphed somebody!" Vestry barked.

He stewed over the bad news. That blasted Josiah and the Freedom Press! That boy and the print shop could ruin his plans!

Vestry rubbed his chin. He had to keep Lucius confident while solving his bigger problem at the same time.

"What if the Klan finds out what we're doing?" Lucius asked.

Waylan calmly crossed the room to the suit of armor. He flipped the helmet's visor, reached in and pulled out the map.

"We could expect swift and violent retaliation," he answered truthfully. Vestry opened the map and rolled it open over his desk, then turned and looked Lucius in the eye.

"So we must work quickly to keep the Klan from discovering who we are. Josiah is a traitor to our cause and the cause of all freedmen. Now our necks are on the line."

Lucius stood very still.

Vestry removed an ink blotter and a small circular stamp from his desk drawer. He opened the blotter and pressed the wooden stamp into the bright red ink.

"Josiah and the Freedom Press will be the cause of our deaths and the deaths of many freedmen if they are not stopped."

Vestry leaned over the map and found the intersection of Chestnut and Sixth. He pressed the stamp carefully onto the map—right where the Freedom Press was located. The map had a new red circle.

Watching Lucius' face closely for a reaction, he leaned over and blew lightly on the fresh ink.

"I can't make these hard decisions by myself, Lucius," Vestry pleaded. "I need your support for what must be done."

Mixed emotions painted Lucius' face. Sad but angry eyes moved from Vestry down to the map, then back up to Vestry. After hesitating several moments, he nodded in agreement.

Vestry put the stamp and blotter away. "Since Josiah is one of your people, I won't ask you to be involved. I'll speak to our backers about how I believe we need to handle the situation. Then once Josiah and the Freedom Press have been dealt with, we can continue with our plans."

After making sure the red ink was dry, Vestry rolled up the map and slipped it back inside the suit of armor. With his back to a silent Lucius, Vestry could barely hold back a chuckle.

* * *

Toby sipped the last of his coffee.

Elbows on the table and his fork dangling between his fingers, Josiah picked at his dinner. The pressure of the day stole over him. For good or bad, Toby and Christine were now implicated in his terrible crime. If Sam couldn't work things out when he got back from Washington, they could all be arrested!

His cheeks burned with shame. Josiah felt the tiny scar above his eye, all that remained from his fisticuffs with Adam Vestry. Inside him, he knew there were other scars too, not scars made by fists or stones, but scars made by every bad decision he had made the last couple of days.

The image of a sweat-drenched and soot-covered Christine, sitting in the dirt with her father's head resting in her lap, framed by their burning home, was but one of several memories that would stay with him and haunt his dreams.

Rising from his chair, Toby carried his cup and dishes to the kitchen. He paused at the table on the way down the hall. "I won't be back from the publishers association meeting until late."

Josiah nodded and lifted a bite of potato to his mouth.

"Just remember," Toby continued, raising his voice as he entered his bedroom, "all's not lost. Sam's got the mayor's ear and Senator Scott's, too. And knowing Sam the way I do, he'll do everything he can to turn a bad situation into good."

Toby passed by and patted him firmly on the shoulder.

"Good night, son," he said in a caring tone. "See you around ten if you're still up."

Then he was gone, his boots bounding noisily down the stairs. Josiah heard the front door open and close as Toby went out.

Josiah rose from the table and returned to his room. He dropped into the chair at his desk, then reached for his new pen.

But the words that wanted to spill onto the blank page of the journal in front of him could not get past the guilt that weighed like a millstone around his heart.

All the trouble he'd caused! The hurt! The fear! The hair on his arms stood on end as Josiah reached and turned off the lamp.

Fear. Josiah knew what fear was all about.

Ten years ago he had struggled awake on a thin layer of hay, his back on the ground. A dark silhouette loomed above him, ringed by the red-orange flames of a burning barn.

Still stunned by the fall from his father's arms, Josiah remembered trying to push himself up. As he did, he could still feel the sensation of a cold ring of steel pressing against the center of his forehead, followed by the loud click of the hammer being drawn.

Josiah's vision cleared as he found himself staring right into the barrel of a rifle. His blood ran cold.

The shadow-faced man glanced briefly back to the other two riders. What happened next, Josiah was not really sure. There had been loud shouts and the harsh crack of firearms going off. Horses brayed, followed by the clop and rumble of hooves. A spray of dirt stung his face. A wide tower of flames roared wildly, consuming the barn and his parents' bodies.

Josiah opened his eyes and focused on a streetlight outside his bedroom window. The memory slowly faded.

Not only had he watched his parents burn to death, but he had also been forced to stare death in the face at the hand of one of the bounty hunters hired by his former owner, Jake Crawford.

And now, because of his mistakes, would Toby and Angelina and other innocent freedmen suffer a similar, frightening fate?

At the edge of his vision, Josiah saw the gleam of the pen Toby had given him, and just beyond the pen, the box it had come in. The box and note, Toby's note. Josiah pulled it free from the box and unfolded it on the desk.

> *Let us hear the conclusion of the whole matter: Fear God, and keep his commandments: for this is the whole duty of man. For God shall bring every work into judgment, with every secret thing, whether it be good, or whether it be evil.*

All the things that Angelina, Daniel and Toby had been trying to warn him about were true!

Josiah clutched the note in his hand, lowered his head to his arms and wept before the only one who could hear him.

20

Adam carefully peered around the edge of the open door into the stable.

Under soft yellow lantern light, he watched his father saddle a horse. Whistling merrily, Waylan stuffed a long coil of rope into a saddlebag. He pulled his Colt revolver from the holster on his hip, then opened and slowly rotated the cylinder, checking each of the six chambers. Smiling, he snapped the cylinder back in place and slid the revolver back into the holster.

"Well, Flint," Waylan said softly, briskly rubbing his black stallion's neck, "hope you're up for a little excitement. The den's not even official yet and we're going to have our first necktie party. It's time to be going; Jed and Tany'll be waiting for us at the Crossroads."

Waylan chuckled, turned off the lamp, and then led Flint toward the open door.

Adam darted silently around the shadowed corner of the stable.

After closing the stable door, Waylan glanced up. Patchwork clouds moved swiftly across a starry sky. A half-moon climbed over the trees.

Whistling again, Waylan slipped his left foot into the stirrup and pulled himself up into the saddle.

"He-ah!" With a tug on the reins, Waylan spun Flint about.

Adam flattened himself against the stable wall as his father rode down the path toward the back of the property.

A den? A necktie party? Jed and Tany? Adam knew them! They were two, tough-nosed, hard-drinking delivery managers who worked for the *Ledger*. And even most pertinent, they were outspoken against blacks.

Adam ran to the front of the stables and flung open the door. He ran to the stall where his own black steed, Rook, neighed with anticipation.

As he quickly saddled his horse, his suspicions hardened into painful fact. His father's secret hatred of blacks, two burly and bigoted Southerners, the map, and now Jed and Tany.

The facts all pointed to one conclusion: his father was involved with the Klan!

Reins in hand, Adam leapt onto Rook. He ducked his head and guided his steed out of the stable.

The Crossroads was where his father was headed. Just north of town, the Crossroads was near the Buck homestead, the Second Methodist Church of Philadelphia and its rectory!

For a moment, Adam felt dizzy.

Everything fit together. The Buck's house, the church and the rectory—all had been circled in red ink on his father's hidden map! And the freedman Lucius—his father had manipulated him for his own ends!

Kicking up dead leaves and sod, Rook responded to the sharp prodding of Adam's boot and galloped down the moonlit path away from the stable.

Loud knocking on the front door beneath his bedroom window caused Josiah to lift his head from his arms. He opened the window and leaned out. Directly below, a young man his own age stood on the sidewalk, staring into the large window.

"What do you want?" Josiah asked.

"Alexander's Messenger Service, here. Got a message for someone named a Mr. Washington. Is he here?"

"I'm Josiah Washington."

The messenger held up a plain white envelope. "Well, do you want it or not?"

"Oh, sorry!" Josiah answered. He closed the window and hurried downstairs.

He opened the front door and stepped out onto the walk. The messenger handed him the envelope, nodded, then turned and headed away.

Josiah went back inside as he tore open the envelope. He unfolded a short handwritten note.

> *Please meet me at the rectory property as soon as possible tonight. I have an urgent and important discovery to show you. Christine.*

He read the note a second time. An urgent discovery? Meet her at the property? Why?

Sitting on a stool, Josiah glanced outside at the darkness and shook his head. What could be so important that they had to meet so late at night?

Josiah folded the note and stuck it into his pocket.

One thing was sure; he was not going to let her stand outside all night waiting for him—not after all she'd done for him!

Waylan Vestry and his two associates reined in their horses behind a thick stand of pine trees. He raised his hand and signaled them to stop as the half-moon peeked out from behind two clouds.

"OK, men! Remember, this isn't the South. I run a tight den. I've got standards: no cussing or mocking the subject. We'll keep everything businesslike. We'll string him up fast and high, then cut him down and bury him. Right now, we can't afford to have his body show up. Any questions?"

The two burly deliverymen shook their heads.

"All right," Waylan said excitedly, his hand dropping to his saddlebag. He lifted the flap and yanked out a robe. "It's time to get dressed for the show."

* * *

Riding through Philadelphia at night in Angelina's buggy on a secret mission fired Josiah's emotions into high gear. What had Christine discovered? Something that linked Lucius to the blaze?

The minutes passed quickly as the buggy rumbled out of the city into rolling farmland that Josiah now knew by heart. Off to his far left on a low rise were the remains of Jason Buck's farmhouse. To his immediate left was the large apple orchard that spread all the way from the Crossroads just ahead to the property where the Methodist church and the rectory had stood.

Clouds moved above in dark bands of gray and black, spangled with alternating rows of twinkling stars. The moon slid in and out from behind the bands.

As Josiah neared the Crossroads, the still-rising moon broke clear and bathed the rutted roads with silver light. Turning Angelina's filly to the left, he bounced noisily through a shallow cut in the road, then rounded the corner at the edge of the apple orchard. Straightening out, he headed in the direction of the rectory property.

To his left, the tidy rows of carefully spaced apple trees stretched into the distance as far as his eye could see in the darkness. To his right, dense stands of tall pines rose above him, casting ragged shadows across the road in front of Angelina's filly.

A quarter of a mile farther down, an opening in the trees appeared on the right. Josiah turned right onto the narrow road that led up an incline between the dark pines to the rectory, or what was left of it.

Josiah's shame returned and spread rapidly across his cheeks as the filly climbed the slope. Coming back to the scene of the crime was more difficult than he thought it would be.

As the filly neared the Y in the road that angled right to the house and left through more pines to the church, Josiah lifted his head. The overwhelming smell of charred rubble sickened him. His eyes shifted from left to right, following the curve of the road up from the pines. In his mind, he saw himself, as he had been clothed the night before, in a black robe and hood, running, staggering up the slope and around the bend, gasping for breath.

Following his memories, Josiah's eyes followed the road up to the top of the hill where the rectory had stood with bright red-orange flames licking out of open windows to the roof and sky.

Then suddenly, his blood ran cold.

Backdropped by the banded, cloudy sky, three horsemen sat motionless in the road on the crest of the hill. Both men and horses had pointed white hoods and flowing white robes that shifted with the breeze and gleamed in the moonlight like spirits from Hell itself.

Angelina's filly sensed the evil too, neighing as Josiah slowed the buggy at the Y in the road.

His eyes scanned the three Klansmen. The one on the right had a coil of rope in his free hand, and the one in the center held a long-barreled pistol across his chest.

An impulse shot down Josiah's arms to the reins.

"Ya! Ya!" he cried, snapping the filly into a gallop down the Y toward the pine-covered opening that led to the church.

As the buggy bounded jarringly down the road, Josiah glanced over his shoulder. The flapping white shapes on the hill behind him had broken into a gallop, too. Josiah knew that he could not outrun the horsemen for long.

The filly and buggy careened down the road between the tall pines. The moon vanished behind a swiftly moving cloud.

The road and trees darkened abruptly. Shadows deepened. Josiah held back a cry as he lost his bearings, the reins loosening in his hands. Undaunted, the filly rushed recklessly ahead into the inky gloom.

Josiah heard loud cursing behind him. Without looking back, he knew the moon's sudden disappearance had slowed the Klansmen as well.

Bouncing over humps and dips in the road, the buggy felt

like it would rattle apart. How the filly kept her speed and balance, Josiah did not know.

Then, with a rush of wind in his face, the buggy struck a bump and rocketed out of the dark mouth of the pines. Josiah braced himself as the buggy came back down to earth with a bone jarring thud. The filly stayed in the center of the road, her hooves pounding the dry dirt down a mild slope toward another thick stand of pines separating the church property from the main road. Across a wide circle of blackened grass to his right, Josiah caught a blurry glimpse the church's ashen remains.

Then the sound of hoofbeats and urging voices behind him warned Josiah the distance between him and his pursuers was closing fast. He glanced over his shoulder.

The Klansmen's long white robes flapped madly in the wind. The charging stallions were less than thirty feet away!

As Josiah snapped his head back around, the buggy's front left wheel broke apart. The buggy pitched forward, careening abruptly to the left, its front corner catching the soft soil just to the left of the road.

The filly's harness and lines snapped loose from the buggy as it stood up on end and launched an unsuspecting Josiah through the air and off to the side into the field.

The sound of splintering wood and twisting metal rent the air as Josiah tumbled into the high grass. The filly stumbled, neighing loudly, then climbed to her feet and galloped down the road and through the dark opening in the pines.

The Klansmen circled the upturned wagon. One wheel spun slowly and noisily.

Stunned but unhurt, Josiah pulled himself to his knees. He shook his head and peered up through the grass. The Klansmen, less than ten feet away, continued to circle their snorting horses around the wagon.

The one nearest him held a long-barreled revolver in his right hand.

Josiah's legs did not hesitate. He scrambled to his feet. Keeping himself low to the ground, he quickly worked his way downhill from the wrecked buggy.

Seconds later, the moon shone through from behind the breaking clouds.

He was three-quarters of the way to the pines when a voice cried out.

"There he is, the little fool!"

Josiah broke into a mad run, legs churning, arms pumping. The voice! He knew the voice of the man calling out!

It was Waylan Vestry!

He heard the rumble of hoofs as he neared the pines. Fear shot down through his legs. Only five paces to go!

Then he was running between the thick pine trees.

Cursing explosively, Vestry pulled hard on the reins and slowed his stallion. He glanced up at the clearing sky, then back to Jed.

He waved his revolver. "Follow him in and force him out! We'll catch him on the far side of the stand! The darkness can't hide him now!"

The Klansman nodded, adjusted his hood, and then goaded his horse into the forest.

Vestry dug his heels into his horse's side. The two Klansmen stormed across the grass to their right and onto the road cutting through the pines.

Some thirty feet away, Josiah leaned with his back against a tree, breathing hard with one hand pressed to his painfully sore ribs. He listened to Waylan Vestry bark a command.

They were going to trap him!

Josiah pushed away from the tree and stumbled forward through the underbrush in the direction of the road. Seconds later, he heard the loud crash of a horseman entering the woods behind him.

He tore himself free from a thorn bush and stumbled into the grass beside the main road bordering the apple orchard. Tall dark pines loomed above him.

"Josiah!" a nearby voice called. "It's me! Adam! Give me your hand!"

Spinning around, Josiah found himself less than five feet from a prancing black steed ridden by Adam Vestry.

Leaning over in the saddle, Adam extended his arm. Moonlight and shadows laced his terror-filled face. "Come on! It's now or never!"

Josiah grabbed his hand. With Adam's help he pulled himself up at the same moment his former enemy spurred his horse into a gallop. Wrapping his arms tightly around Adam's waist, he hung on as the horse sprinted across the road into the apple orchard.

Looking over their shoulders, Adam and Josiah saw two white-robed horsemen break out of the opening in the dark green pines several hundred feet farther down the road. At the same time, a third exited the forest where Josiah had stood just moments before.

Adam turned around and urged Rook on with a prod of his heels. "Duck!" he cried, as he crossed from one row of trees to another.

"Again!"

Josiah slouched quickly a second time as Adam slanted into yet another open row. Budding branches brushed the top of his hair.

Rook snorted and leapt a narrow ditch. Josiah bounced on the steed's hard rump, grimacing.

Now they were crossing a narrow, tilled field. Fifty yards to their left stood a farmhouse. Light glowed from windows in the front. Moments later, Adam turned Rook down a footpath through another stand of trees.

"Whoa, boy," he said into his horse's ear, pulling back on the reins. Adam turned him again sharply to the right. Snorting softly with his sides heaving, Rook slowed to a halt in a deep shadow beneath a tall and spreading elm tree.

Josiah slid off the horse to the ground. Rubbing his backside, he stepped away to face Adam and his horse.

"I don't think they'll find us here," Adam explained quietly as he dismounted. He patted Rook on the shoulder and rubbed his neck. "We're smack between two houses and there's no way they can see us behind this row of trees. Beside, I don't think they really want to be seen."

"Why did you save me?" Josiah blurted, his breath coming in heaves. He wondered if Adam knew his father was one of the Klansmen chasing them.

Adam walked around his horse and leaned against the elm. Josiah could not make out Adam's expression in the darkness.

"Do you want to know the truth? I couldn't let my father and his men go through with it."

Josiah gasped.

"For the last few days," Adam continued, his voice softening, "I've been spying on him. He's not too good at hiding things when he's excited.

"So tonight, I followed him out. From the apple grove I saw him and his men ride up the road to the reverend's house. A little while later, you rambled by in a buggy and turned up the same road. That's when I really started worrying.

"I stayed down by the road and worked my way along the pines. Not long after I heard the crash, I heard my father calling out, but believe me, I was as surprised to see you tonight as you were to see me!"

Adam pushed himself away from the elm. Beams of moonlight broken by the tree limbs illumined his face in silvery bands. Josiah could tell that deep, conflicting emotions tore at him.

The two young men stood five feet apart.

"I don't know where all this is going to lead," Adam said, shaking his head.

"My dad is a powerful man. And I'm not sure who else is in

this with him. I don't think he saw me, but if he did, I'm in danger too. We're dealing with the Klan and I don't know if my dad can—." Adam paused, his eyes lowering and hating the words that came from his mouth, "or would be willing to protect me."

"We both need to talk to Toby," Josiah suggested, taking a step forward. "He'll have an idea about what we should do."

"I guess we're in this together, then?" Adam's voice was tentative. He took a step forward and extended a hand. "I admit I did you wrong. Can you forget about what happened that day behind the State House?"

Josiah studied Adam's hand. This Adam Vestry seemed very different from the ruffian who had punched him and called him names.

He reached out slowly and accepted Adam's hand.

"All right. I can forget the fists and the stones."

21

After brushing Flint down, Waylan Vestry led the horse to his stall. He filled a bucket with oats and set it on the floor in the corner. Dawn was still two hours away. His thoughts, however, were not on the well-being of his stallion this early Sunday morning.

Boiling with anger, he scooped up the saddlebags from the floor and tossed them on the stand near the wall. His bloodshot eyes darted to the empty stall where Rook should have been.

In his mind, Vestry could still see the momentary glimpse of Josiah, his arms wrapped around a hunkered-down rider on a swiftly moving dark horse, disappearing into the apple orchard. Pursuit had been short and futile. The horsemen had headed straight for the nearby Bligh homestead and then vanished.

Dressed in Klan garb, Waylan and his men had been forced to turn back and let Josiah and his rescuer escape.

Vestry fired a foul curse into the night air and slammed his left fist into his right palm.

His eyes moved again to the empty stall next to Flint's. So, Adam and Rook were out. Where and with whom was the question. Hopefully, he had not been riding anywhere near the Crossroads. That would be one complication he really didn't want to have to deal with!

Things were getting messy. And with Jennings and Crawford due back tomorrow, 'messy' was a dangerous word!

* * *

Josiah led a worried Toby down a straw-littered row of stalls at Morton's Livery and Hack Stable. Morton's was located a block south of the Freedom Press.

Lantern light cast shadows and exaggerated the sharp lines in Toby's normally smooth features. Concern bunched around his tired eyes and the corners of his mouth.

"Took us a while, but we found Angelina's filly," Josiah explained quietly. "We can get the buggy tomorrow, but it's so busted up I don't think even Honest Abe could fix it."

At the far end of the stable, Adam stopped brushing Rook and turned around as Toby and Josiah approached. Nearby, Angelina's filly munched on an unbound sheaf of oats.

"So, Adam," Toby said in a hushed voice, placing his hands on his hips and surveying the situation, "Josiah tells me you saved his life."

"Yes, I believe so." Adam glanced at Josiah, then back to Toby.

Josiah, chewing lightly on his lower lip, nodded. His eyes narrowed slightly.

Toby studied Josiah's face, then returned his sober stare to Adam. "Did any of them recognize you or your horse?"

Adam brushed his hair from his eyes and swallowed hard. "I hope not. We'd just cut into the Bligh's orchard. They were a good ways off."

Rubbing his chin, Toby let out a long sigh. "I guess it's fair to figure that Josiah's gotten himself in some deep trouble. It doesn't make a lot of sense, but it seems to me that the Klan is mixed up with that outfit led by Lucius, only I doubt that Lucius and his men know who they're serving."

Josiah eyed Adam and pressed his lips together tightly. He and Adam had already put that much together. Waylan was using Lucius to do his dirty work against the families who had been working for freedmen's rights.

Now Josiah wondered if Adam's request to keep the truth about his father quiet for a few days was a good idea. But they had agreed, and Josiah was not about to break his word with the one who had saved his life.

"We've got to decide what we're going to do," Toby continued. "After church, we'll meet with Christine. And since we don't know who's who, we've got to be real careful what we say and whom we say it to."

Toby put a hand on Josiah's shoulder. "Sam, Angelina and the mayor are coming back on the train Monday night. We've got to pray that things stay calm until then."

Shadows cast by the amber lantern light masked the dread that crept over Josiah's and Adam's faces.

The Second Methodist Church of Philadelphia held its Sunday meetings in a barn less than a quarter mile from the burned-out rubble of its original site.

From his bed in the farmhouse adjacent to the barn, Pastor Thompson listened to the singing. The joy his congregation normally expressed in their worship service had been replaced with somber reflection. Suspicions ran high, and fears of riots and racial unrest occupied the people's thoughts.

At eleven the service came to a close. Christine, who had been staring out the window by her father's bed, watched the last of the families leave the barn. She rose from her chair.

Standing in the doorway, Josiah studied the Reverend Thompson's tired but serene face. Coming with Christine to meet with her father had been Toby's idea, so Josiah could ask forgiveness and demonstrate his commitment to do what was right.

Josiah had been surprised and humbled by the forgiveness he had found. Even though the reverend's voice was weak, the meaning of his words had been clear and his logic certain, just as Toby's had been the night before. Wrong was wrong but mercy, he had said, needed to prevail. What counted most now was discovering the identities of the men manipulating Lucius. Evil was afoot, threatening the fragile relationship between whites and freedmen.

"We'll be going, Father," she said, gently squeezing his hand.

"We need to meet with Toby."

The reverend nodded, met Josiah's gaze briefly with a thin smile, then closed his eyes.

Outside, they met Toby by the horse and carriage her father had borrowed from a neighbor. Angelina's filly stood tethered to a tree nearby.

Toby grabbed the filly's line and untied it. "Josiah, you drive the carriage with Christine. I'll follow."

Five minutes later, Josiah turned the carriage up a narrow dirt road in front of the apple orchard. The road was halfway between two farms and ran down to an unnamed, half-acre sunfish pond. The pond could not be seen from the road.

Josiah slowed the carriage to a halt. Toby dismounted from Angelina's filly and let her graze.

"Who are we meeting?" Christine asked as Josiah helped her down from the carriage.

No sooner had she asked the question, than a rider on a handsome black steed appeared from a row of apple trees on the other side of the pond.

"Adam Vestry?" she asked, her cheeks blushing unexpectedly.

"He saved my life," Josiah answered simply, looking at Adam as he rounded the left side of the pond and approached them.

Christine's eyes sparkled, darting from Josiah to Toby and then to Adam as he slid from the saddle to the ground.

"Toby. Josiah. A pleasure to see you again, Miss Thompson," Adam offered politely, nodding his head and tipping his cap. "Shouldn't we get down to business?"

Toby stepped forward. "Christine, it's time you heard the whole story."

"Yes, I suppose it is," she said, her eyes never leaving Adam.

Waylan Vestry stared out the window on the backside of the Public Ledger Building looking down into the alley. Below him, Lucius Morris had just entered Horner's Insurance Agency through a rear window. Vestry remembered the last time he had visited Tom Horner. A narrow back room opened into an equally narrow interior, jam-packed with file cabinets and desks. Tom always kept the office's front window blinds closed.

Vestry sighed deeply. In spite of his plans going a slight bit askew, Lucius had continued to accept his lies, to the point of accepting the fact that he needed to burn down the Freedom Press! He envisioned Lucius dumping a stack of papers on the floor, then lighting a match and dropping it onto the pile. In moments, the chairs and desks would be ablaze. Five minutes and the whole place would be up in flames.

A whiff of smoke passed through the back window and into the alley. Lucius had completed his job!

Out of the corner of his eye, Vestry noticed a wagon turn the corner and head down the street. He cursed.

The wagon was full of freedmen dressed in their Sunday best.

Toby tugged on the reins and turned the carriage onto Sixth Street. Josiah, sitting on the opposite end of the seat, glanced to his left and studied Christine's face. Something about her had changed after their meeting with Adam by the pond.

Her intense sadness and pain had lessened, but there was something else: a new gleam in her eyes and a mouth that edged easily into a smile.

As they approached the intersection of Sixth and Chestnut, Josiah's eyes rose to the tall white tower and bell atop the State House. He realized that Adam and Christine were not the only ones who had changed. Another change had occurred as well, a change inside of him.

"Josiah! Look!" Christine cried out, startling him. She grabbed his arm. Toby gasped loudly as Josiah spun in the seat.

Dark smoke curled out the front door and windows of the insurance agency adjacent to the Freedom Press. A dozen or more blacks and several whites scurried back and forth between two freight wagons. Four women stood in the back of the otherwise empty wagons and watched.

Toby clucked his tongue and snapped the reins, urging the horse around the corner. Josiah stood up in the moving carriage. Moments later, Toby pulled over and stopped directly across the street from the Freedom Press.

Josiah jumped from the carriage and helped Christine down. A short man with a cigar hanging from his mouth intercepted Toby as he crossed the street.

Honest Abe raised his hands. Smoke from the insurance agency curled toward the sky behind him.

"Everything's OK! Your shop's safe. Ten minutes ago, me and my boys were on our way back from church when ol' man Lender, my wife's father, stopped the wagons. He's blind as a bat but has the nose of a beagle. Claimed he smelled smoke. Then my wife pointed her finger at Tom Horner's office window.

"Tom and you and others on this block can thank God he gave her father such a nose!"

Toby thanked Abe and shook his hand firmly. About that time, a fire engine from the East Side Pump and Ladder rumbled around the corner by the State House and Public Ledger Building. Eight anxious firemen stood on long sideboards and clung to the engine.

"Now they show up!" Abe laughed. "Don't fret yourself, Toby. I'll handle 'em. I know two of the men at Eastside."

Toby, Josiah, and Christine hurried across the street and entered the Freedom Press. The smell of smoke was strong, but the air was breathable. Fifteen minutes later, a quick but thorough search revealed no damage to the print shop on either floor.

Sitting on stools in the production room on the ground floor, Josiah and Christine sipped from glasses filled with water. They watched Honest Abe, a distraught Tom Horner, and Toby converse with the captain of the Eastside Pump and Ladder.

Christine looked Josiah in the eyes. "So, don't you think it's time to tell them who's behind all this?"

"I can't," Josiah answered, glancing down. "I promised Adam.

He wants a chance to talk to his father. Then, if that doesn't work, he agrees that we have no choice but to turn him in. One more day—that's all Adam asked for."

Josiah lifted his eyes at last. They were filled with worry. "Just one more day."

22

Not only did the Horner's Insurance Agency make headline news, but so did a third fire on the ridge north of town. Bill Corbin, an opponent of freedmen's rights, lost a barn. The article stated that Bill was quick to cast blame at "vengeful Negroes" who were "quickly reverting to the basic instincts of their lower nature."

Monday morning's edition of the *Public Ledger*, known for its refusal to publish unfounded speculation, nonetheless joined with the increasingly popular view that "issues of race" were indeed at the root of the evil underfoot in Philadelphia. Arson was the only plausible explanation for the fires. One accidental fire was believable; two on two consecutive nights stretched reason; three fires, three nights in a row pressed all probabilities.

Josiah watched Toby fold the newspaper and set it on the table.

"I don't think the insurance agency was their real target." Toby's eyes drooped with worry. "I think they were after the Freedom Press."

He reached for his coffee cup and glanced across at Josiah who, once again, picked at his food. "Son, you can't blame yourself for what happened to Reverend Thompson or the church or Jason Buck's house or any of this. Yesterday evening, when we took Christine home, you heard her say she doesn't hold you responsible. She's right—same fires would've burned whether you'd been there or not."

Rising from his chair, Toby entered the kitchen.

Josiah pulled the newspaper in front of him. His smooth oval face creased with anger as he scanned the headlines. Waylan Vestry, the man behind all of the trouble, wrote one of the articles!

Toby set his plate and cup in a pot of water and continued speaking. Out of the corner of his eye, he watched Josiah brooding over the paper.

"I'm going to the telegraph office," Toby explained as he dried his hands on a towel, "then to Honest Abe's. We have an emergency meeting at the Freedman's Relief Association over on Walnut Street. Philadelphia's ready to explode. If another house or building burns, I don't know if the truth about Lucius and his outfit will make any difference at all. The only thing that will end this crisis is finding out the names of the Klansmen controlling Lucius."

Pushing the newspaper away from him, Josiah forced a bite of cold pancake into his mouth. As Toby crossed the room, Josiah avoided his eyes.

"Keep yourself busy and don't fret," Toby said from the stairs. "The presses need a thorough cleaning and the floors haven't been swept since last Friday. Just stay inside today, for your own safety. We don't know what those Klansmen will try next."

"Yes, sir," Josiah replied. "Just as you say."

Toby forced a smile, then disappeared down the stairs.

Waylan Vestry closed the door to his office behind the two broad-shouldered Southerners.

"Well, gentlemen, I hope you're pleased with the developments here in Philadelphia."

Jennings, who moved to stand by the window, lightly nodded his head. He shot a glance at Crawford who plopped himself into a side chair to the left of the suit of armor. The chair creaked beneath his huge frame.

"Everything seems to be going as planned," Crawford replied with his deep-voiced Georgia drawl. "On the surface."

Vestry cleared his throat. "What could possibly be wrong? This city is primed and ready to be turned to the Klan's noble cause of chivalry, humanity, mercy and patriotism."

"Yes, I would agree," Crawford answered. "But what troubles Jennings and me are the newspaper reports that it's colored reprisals against whites that's stirring everybody up. Now, you wouldn't be having anything to do with using stinkin' coloreds to do your Klan work, would you?"

Vestry felt the blood begin to drain from his face. He knew he had to act fast or his reaction was going to give him away.

He strode across the room. He sucked in a deep breath, twisted his face up in anger and hammered his fist on the map that lay face up and open across his desk.

"Of course not! I don't even talk to them unless business forces me to."

Feeling the mounting pressure of his lies, he stared Crawford straight in the eyes and hoped his ploy would work.

The burly Southerner maintained his gaze, then shifted his eyes to his partner by the window. "Let's give our compatriot the good news."

Crawford leaned against the doorway. He placed his arms across his chest. Eyebrows arching, he refocused his penetrating gaze on Vestry.

Jennings pulled a telegram out of his jacket pocket. "Our contacts in Washington have confirmed tonight's target. This is our chance to remove Senator Scott, the mayor of Philadelphia, and that pesky Freedom Press publisher in one blow."

Excitement surged through Waylan. The news was too good to be true! At last, Sam MacDonald would be out of his way! And once he was gone, the Freedom Press would fold like a house of cards.

Jennings' face brightened as he turned his gaze from the telegram to the map with the red circles.

"Tomorrow, when the city of Philadelphia is greeted by a brand new day, they will also be met by the glorious rising of the Ku Klux Klan."

* * *

Adam led Rook out of his stall. He reached for his saddle, threw it onto his horse's back and adjusted the strap.

As he placed his foot into the stirrup and pulled himself up onto Rook, he wondered how Christine would react to his unannounced visit. He prodded his horse out into the street.

Christine Thompson. He had liked her ever since the seventh grade, and it seemed that she liked him, too. But what did she think of him now that the truth about his father had been revealed? Would she still want to be his friend?

What was it about her that made him feel the way he did? Was it her pretty face? Her long hair? Was it her sometimes stormy eyes?

Yes, she was nice to look at. But there was more to Christine than looks. She was a good person through and through, a little naive, but determined. And it was her determination that set her apart from the other young women he had known.

She and her father were very close. Perhaps that was where her strength came from. That was something he could only long for with his own father.

Adam shook his head and wondered just how all of this was going to work out. As Rook bore him to the edge of town and the farm where Christine and her father were staying, he offered a quiet prayer.

"God, please help us all. I'm sure you know more than we do just how much we need your help."

The unplanned request felt strange, almost clumsy. Adam Vestry had not prayed for a long, long time.

Adam dismounted and tied Rook to the hitching post. Head low, he ambled up wooden steps and crossed the porch to the farm house door. He knocked three times and turned around, facing the downward slope of the hill overlooking Philadelphia.

He heard the door open, then Christine's questioning voice.

"Adam, what are you doing here?"

He turned around and removed his hat, placing it over his chest. Their eyes met briefly but then Adam looked away.

"Christine, may I speak with you for a moment?"

Christine stepped outside and closed the door behind her. Side by side, they stepped down from the porch and walked out across the sloping hill, stopping halfway and looking out at the greening trees and the north edge of the city.

"It's hard to face that my father is in so deep with the Klan," Adam said softly without looking at her. He could sense that she was looking at him, studying him. The track of a tear marked his cheek.

Running her hand through her hair and flipping it back over her shoulders, Christine nodded.

Then he turned toward her and their eyes met again.

Adam had never stood so close to Christine, not even at their seventh grade dance. For the first time, he noticed how her eyes had more green in them than blue, how the thin band of freckles splashed across her cheeks and nose, and how her hair sprang softly from a widow's peak.

He wanted to take her hand in his, only he knew that now was not the right time.

"You know," he said, fumbling for words, "my fight with Josiah was partly about you. My pride got the best of me. At first I was just showing off, but then I couldn't back down. I was wrong for what I did and I told Josiah so. Now I'm telling you this because I want you to know that I don't want to end up like my father."

Christine breathed deeply. "I believe you."

Encouraged, Adam swallowed hard and pressed on.

"And when we get through this crisis and things settle down, I'd like to ask your father if I could call on you. I know that now's just not the time."

Christine pressed her lips together thoughtfully. A breeze rustled her long curls.

"I understand," she said softly. Then after a moment's hesitation she added, "I would really like that. I think Papa will agree."

Adam turned and looked back toward Philadelphia. What should have been one of the most enjoyable afternoons of his life was marred by uncertainty. Images of brandished guns, white hoods and robes and burning crosses played though his mind. For Christine's sake, he fought back the frown that had started to form on his face.

Where would trouble spring up next?

And when?

Evening came with a cool breeze gusting down from the northwest. Vestry and his associates, Jed and Tany, waited in lantern light by the open stable behind his house.

No hoods or robes tonight. They were all dressed in blacks and browns. Crawford had been specific.

"When they goin' to get here?" Tany asked, fingering the pistol holstered at his side.

"Not they—he." Vestry corrected as he spun the cylinder and checked each chamber of his long-barreled Colt. "Only Crawford. Jennings is on his way back to Georgia."

Tany's face folded into a frown. "Think we need more help for Ellard's Crossing? Sounds like we got a whole load of work to do."

A deep voice behind the stand of pine trees to the right of the stable startled the three men.

"You boys look like you'll do just fine for tearing up a little stretch of track," Crawford growled. He stepped into the light with his horse in tow.

Vestry reholstered his pistol and took a deep breath. Jed and Tany, who had never met Crawford before, stepped forward and tentatively extended their hands. Though Jed and Tany were big men, they were still half a head shorter than the burly southerner.

Crawford ignored them and tethered his horse to the open

stable door. Jed and Tany lowered their hands and stepped back toward the edge of the shadows.

Vestry stepped forward. "Everything's set. All the tools you requested have been distributed evenly, just like you asked. We'll be able to ride hard and fast. Tomorrow, Philadelphia will wake up to one of the most violent tragedies in its history and to one that we'll pin squarely on the coloreds."

Crawford nodded, entered the stable, and started checking the horses and the saddlebags for himself.

As Jed and Tany looked on, movement on the path behind the pines caused Vestry to turn his head. He did a double take, then spun around. The hairs on his neck stood on end.

Lucius Morris walked casually into the light for their seven o'clock meeting which Vestry had forgotten to cancel.

"Waylan, weren't we supposed to meet—" Lucius' words died abruptly on his lips as he saw the shock and anger on his employer's face, and on the faces of the two men standing behind him in the glowing lantern light.

"What in the blazes!" Tany exclaimed, his eyes moving rapidly between the wide-eyed black man and the others.

Lucius started to turn but then lurched to a stop.

Crawford pointed his rifle at Lucius' midsection. "So you do know Mistah Waylan," he asked mockingly. Shaking his head, Crawford cocked the lever to his rifle and pumped a shell into the firing chamber.

Lucius swallowed hard and remained silent.

"You're a dead man," Crawford drawled coldly.

Vestry stepped quickly across the path and pushed down on the barrel of the rifle. "Not on my property, he's not."

Yanking his long-barreled Colt from its holster, Vestry turned and faced Lucius who had broken out in a cold sweat. "Get out of here! Don't ever show your face in Philadelphia again! If you do, I'll be the one to fill your gut with lead."

For a moment, Lucius did not move. Then his legs unlocked and he broke away, crashing through the pine trees to reach the path.

Jed and Tany broke out laughing, then stopped when Crawford turned his head and stared them down. The southerner then faced Vestry, who stood with pistol in hand listening to the sound of Lucius' running feet fade in the distance.

Crawford stepped up until his face was inches away from Vestry's. "Boy, you got something to learn about how the Klan does its business. In Georgia, we'd hang a man for less."

"This isn't Georgia," Vestry countered, mustering courage. Philadelphia was his city, not Crawford's! "If the Klan wants to move north, then the Klan's got to learn a few things itself."

Something hard and ugly in Crawford's eyes made Vestry flinch. Then the next thing he knew, Crawford had backed off and uncocked his rifle.

"All right, let's get on with it!" was all he said.

Vestry shivered and entered the stable to get his horse. As the men mounted their horses, movement behind a thick shrub on the other side of the stable went unnoticed.

With a wave of his arm, Vestry and an angry Crawford led Jed and Tany down the dark path and southward away from the city.

23

With a little extra effort early in the evening, Josiah left the Freedom Press spotless. The presses were clean, shelves of supplies were neatly organized, and the floors were swept.

Thirty minutes later, Josiah sat at the table near the kitchen and ate a bowl of cheese and potato soup for dinner. Toby had already come and gone twice, meeting with other black leaders in and around Philadelphia. Rumors were spreading rapidly, faster than Toby and the others could extinguish. Fear was spreading among both blacks and whites, and nobody was sure how to stop it.

Josiah heard the door to the Freedom Press open and shut, followed by movement across a hardwood floor.

Josiah hurried downstairs.

Adam stood at the counter next to Toby. Adam turned around. Josiah could see the anger tearing his new friend's face and filling his eyes.

"What happened?" Josiah asked, as Toby pulled a stool beneath him and sat down. He looked upset, but restrained himself.

The two young men followed his lead.

"I was just about to tell Toby what just happened," Adam explained. He glanced at Toby, then back to Josiah. "I followed my father out to the stables tonight and hid behind the shrubs."

He recounted what he had seen and overheard: how his father, Jed and Tany had been joined by a Klansman; how Lucius came unexpectedly and how his father grabbed the Klansman's rifle and stopped him from killing Lucius on the spot.

"After my father sent Lucius away, that southerner was steaming mad," Adam explained, shaking his head with concern. "Got right up in his face. Said that my father had something to learn about how the Klan did business—how in Georgia, they'd hang a man for less."

Adam's voice broke. He stared down at the table.

The room grew silent.

Toby closed his eyes and sighed. He then told Adam and Josiah how, ten years earlier, a hatemonger had tried to murder his business partner, Sam MacDonald. Those had been dark, terrible years when evil stalked both North and South, filling thousands upon thousands of souls in both Blue and Gray with a lust for bloodshed. Those were long years when madness filled the land and hatred took the form of cannons, firearms and bayonets.

"I've had a feeling that we're living in one of those times again, and if the Klan gets a foothold here in Philadelphia, then there's nothin' that'll stop them from movin' north. Hatred and bigotry will burn like a brush fire before the wind. Whatever gains of freedom we freedmen have made these last seven years could be lost."

Toby put a firm hand on Adam's forearm. His voice softened. "I'm sorry about your father and what he's gotten himself into. But if the Klan gets a foothold in Philadelphia, then the whole North's next to follow. We've got to stop them. Is there anything else you remember that might give us a clue about what he and his Klansman friend have planned?"

Josiah felt his friend's sadness.

Adam lowered his eyes for a moment, then abruptly looked up. "I do remember one thing. Tany complained about what they were going to do at Ellard's Crossing. They talked about tearing up track. The Crossing is one of the locations my father circled in red on a map I found hidden in his office."

"Tearing up track at Ellard's Crossing," Toby muttered. Then his eyes popped wide open. "They're going to wreck a train! Lord have mercy!"

Toby jumped to his feet, knocking over his stool.

He ran to his room and grabbed his coat. His voice was almost frantic as he opened his pocket watch. "Josiah, you and Adam stay right here! I'm going to find somebody—the Freedmen's Association, the city militia—whoever will believe me. Sam, Angelina and Daniel are on a train coming up from Washington and it's due in an hour!"

Through the large glass window of the shop on the ground floor, Josiah and Adam watched Toby sprint down Chestnut Street. He ran in the direction of the nearby Livery and Hack where his borrowed carriage was housed. For several minutes, Josiah and Adam stared silently out the front window.

"I don't know about Toby's plan," Adam grimaced suddenly. "The more I think about it, the more it worries me. What if help doesn't come quickly? They've got to muster everyone together and get all the way out to Ellard's. That's a hard, twenty-minute ride all by itself. And whoever rides out is going to face one tough bunch. And that southerner Crawford's the vilest man I've ever seen. I think he's the one who got my father to join the Klan."

Numbing cold shot through Josiah's stomach at the name of Crawford. Images tumbled together. His parents working in cotton fields at the plantation in Ellijay, Georgia. Daniel Sweetwater had suffered at the hands of Jake Crawford, too, some twenty years earlier.

Could the very same Crawford be here in Philadelphia?

"I think you may be right. But by now, Toby'll already be on his way." Josiah traced his right index finger over the word FREEDOM painted on the window. Another quiet minute passed, then he looked up, his face suddenly filled with resolve. "We've got to make sure that if Toby doesn't make it in time, somebody does."

Adam fired Josiah a questioning glance.

"Who's somebody?"

* * *

Rook tore across the dirt road and into the grassy field beneath a full moon. The wind snapped at Adam's hair and clothes.

A dozen strides behind Rook, Josiah dug in his heels and hung on as Angelina's filly labored to keep up with the black steed's breakneck pace. The last street of buildings in South Philadelphia was ten minutes behind them.

The long field narrowed suddenly on a steep decline between two tall stands of trees. The filly followed Rook down Adam's shortcut to Ellard's Crossing.

"There they are! On the other side of the bridge!" Adam whispered excitedly as he peered over the tall brush near the edge of the shallow ravine.

Josiah stepped between the row of pines to Adam's side. To their left, the railway bridge stretched less than two hundred feet across rocky, slow-moving Ellard's Creek some ten feet below.

"It isn't fast, but it's deep," Adam explained, pointing, "and if a fast-moving train jumped the tracks, a lot of people will be killed or injured."

"Toby said Sam and Angelina are on the train coming up from Washington. We've got to find a way to stop Crawford and your father."

Adam turned and put his hand on Josiah's shoulder. "There's no way we can stop them directly, but we might be able to stop the train before it reaches the bridge. Then it won't matter what they're doing to the tracks over there. We just need to cross the creek and find a way to signal the train farther down the tracks without them catching on to what we're doing."

Josiah nodded agreement. "Right! We can ride right along the tracks until we meet up with the train."

They slipped quietly through the pines to a rocky path below the railroad embankment where their horses were tethered. As

Adam and Josiah slipped their boots into the stirrups, they heard a loud metallic click behind them.

A man stepped out of the shadows with a rifle in his hands.

"Now move real slow, both of you," Tany warned as he walked cautiously around them to the left.

"Get your feet back on the ground, loose those lines and lead your horses up that hill to the tracks. And don't act brave, or I'll be forced to pump bullets in your backs!"

Tany's face paled as the young man standing next to the black horse turned around. "What'n the blazes? Why, you're Waylan's boy!"

With a wave of his rifle, he motioned his captives up the path to the tracks.

24

A curse split the air.

Adam stared straight down at the moonlit ground. Rook and Angelina's filly pranced uneasily nearby, both tethered to a sturdy sapling to the right of the railroad tracks.

Josiah stood silently to Adam's right, looking down and trying to avoid catching the angry gaze of Jake Crawford. All he could do was hope that his and his parents' former owner did not recognize him. Tension filled the air and tingled the hairs on the back of his neck.

Tany kept his rifle trained on the two young men.

Waylan Vestry, kneeling in the dirt with his shirt sleeves rolled up to his elbows, hung his head and looked down at the sections of track that he had helped tear up. His eyes rose slightly to his coat and holster that hung on a post a couple of feet away.

Jed knelt near the torn-up tracks beside Waylan. He looked at Adam. His mouth fell open in obvious disbelief at the now-complicated situation.

Crawford's face turned fiery red. "Vestry, what a sloppy mess! You're a bigger fool than I imagined!"

Crawford spun to face Adam. Josiah's eyes followed Crawford's hand as his fingers moved menacingly above his holster.

"How'd you two know to follow us here?" the Southerner bellowed.

Adam clenched his teeth and stood silently.

Crawford snarled and backhanded Adam sharply across the mouth. The hard thwack of his knuckles knocked Adam backward. He stumbled, then regained his balance. The blow split his lower lip. Blood spilled down his chin.

Josiah moved toward his friend, but Adam waved him off.

"Doesn't matter," Crawford mumbled as he turned back toward Vestry and his two men.

The burly Klansman drew himself up to his full height. Josiah noticed that though his face looked suddenly calm, his fingers still danced above his holster. He shot a firm look at Tany and Jed. "You two boys slip on outa here. You've done enough. Now that the track work's finished, Vestry and I can handle the rest."

Tany nodded. A few feet behind him, Jed bobbed his head up and down in agreement. From the looks on their faces, Josiah could tell they were anxious to get away.

"Sure enough, Mr. Crawford. Whatever you say."

The two men lowered their rifles and crossed the broken railroad tracks to the clump of maples where their horses stood hidden from the tracks. They slid their rifles into the long, leather sleeves that hung beside their saddlebags.

They climbed into their saddles, reined their horses and started across the narrow railroad bridge toward Philadelphia.

Tany cast a worried glance over his shoulder.

Standing sideways to the bridge, with his feet planted firmly and his hand poised above his holster, Crawford waited until Tany turned back around. He yanked his pistol free and raised it to eye level.

Straight-backed and straight-armed, he sighted his targets and squeezed the trigger.

Josiah and Adam flinched twice at the repeated bark of Crawford's pistol. Rook whinnied and bumped into the equally nervous filly.

Simultaneously, Tany and Jed slumped forward and tumbled from their saddles. Tany fell off the bridge to the left; Jed fell to the right. Their horses kicked up their hooves and broke away across the bridge as the lifeless bodies splashed into the creek below.

Josiah watched Waylan's eyes dart to his gun belt and holster which hung on a post at the side of the bridge.

Adam saw it too but quickly looked away as Crawford turned to face them. He held his pistol in his right hand, an open pocket watch in his left. He grinned fiendishly and snapped the watch shut.

He lifted his head. "Well, Vestry, I guess it's about time for that train of ours to show. And even though you royally messed things up, I think everything's going to turn out just fine!"

Vestry edged backward toward the post. His sweaty white hair gleamed in the moonlight.

"You're not going to shoot my son, are you?" he asked, moving closer to the bridge and the post.

Crawford turned and stared at Adam, his back to Vestry. Crooked teeth showed through an evil smile. "Why, of course, Mistah Waylan. We can't let him live to tell the whole wide world what he knows, can we?"

Vestry reached back and silently pulled his long-barreled Colt out of the holster. With his free hand he wiped his eyes.

Josiah and Adam fought to keep their eyes trained on Crawford.

The Klansman's toothy smile twisted grotesquely as he studied the changing lines of Adam's face. His voice slipped into a heavy drawl.

"Now, you wouldn't be thinkin' about crossin' me again, would you? There're lessons you still haven't learned about the Klan. Just remember now, I warned you."

Vestry squared himself to Crawford's back. "And I warned you! This isn't Georgia! This is my state, my city!"

Crawford's eyes narrowed to thin slits as he broke into a raucous belly laugh.

Vestry raised his Colt. Adam's head snapped towards his father as Crawford whipped around in a blur of unexpected speed. Vestry's Colt only clicked. The chambers were empty!

"No!" Adam screamed, grasping for the Klansman's arm far too late.

Crawford's pistol boomed twice.

Josiah dashed toward the filly. Someone had to warn the train!

Waylan Vestry stared at his Colt in disbelief as two growing red circles appeared in the dead center of his white shirt. His eyes rolled up as he toppled backward into low shrubs at the edge of the ravine.

Crawford deftly sidestepped to his left, lifted his arm and thumped Adam on the back of the head with the butt of his pistol. Adam stumbled across the tracks and pitched forward onto his knees beside his father.

Josiah heard the commotion behind him but did not look back. He ripped the horses' tethers free from the sapling. A fiery pain tore through his left biceps, accompanied by the crack of Crawford's pistol.

He'd been shot!

Now freed, Rook and Angelina's filly bounded away in opposite directions alongside the track.

"Come back here, boy, or I'll drill your friend just like I drilled his old man."

Josiah shook as he turned around. His left biceps burned as though someone had stuck a red hot knife straight into his flesh. He felt a spreading warmth inside his coat sleeve and knew without looking that he had been shot. He clasped his hand over the fiery spot. He grimaced as he stumbled back toward the tracks.

Adam picked up his father's Colt, unlocked the cylinder and spun it slowly.

He looked up with tears in his eyes. "His revolver didn't have any rounds in it."

Keeping his pistol aimed at Adam, Crawford shrugged. "I emptied his pistol while he was working on the tracks. I warned him, fair and square, that the Klan just doesn't put up with his kind of shenanigans."

"Fair and square?" Adam questioned angrily, waving the empty Colt at Crawford. "You set him up, then killed him in cold blood!"

"You've got it all wrong," Crawford mocked with an offended look on his face. "He pulled his gun on me. I was just defending myself. It's not my problem he didn't check to see if the revolver was loaded."

A wordless cry escaped Adam as he flung the Colt at Crawford.

The Klansman raised a forearm and deflected the revolver into the grass.

As Josiah stepped onto the tracks, he sensed a faint rumble beneath his feet. He looked down the steel rails as they curved and disappeared to the right fifty yards away behind a dense stand of trees.

Then, somewhere in the distant darkness, the sharp sound of a steam whistle split the air.

Crawford's voice cracked with excitement. "Here she comes! And nothin's going to stop her now!"

Josiah winced as a searing pang knifed from his upper arm to his shoulder. He could do nothing as the Klansman grabbed Adam by the coat collar, pulled him to his feet and jammed a pistol into his side.

"Let's go! And I mean now! Get moving or I'll blow a hole through your friend!"

Josiah followed them behind the clump of trees where Crawford's and Vestry's steeds stood tethered.

Crawford pushed his pistol harder into Adam's side, forcing him to groan.

"Not a word now, from either of you! Or you're dead!"

Josiah shuddered and continued counting to himself. Crawford had already fired off five shots—one each into Tany and Jed, two into Adam's father and one through his own arm. With only one shot left, Crawford couldn't stop both of them!

A surge of pain up his arm told him whom the Klansman would shoot first. Wounded, Josiah knew that he could not outrun Crawford.

Squeezing his eyes together, Josiah prayed with all his heart that Toby and the militia would arrive and save them.

The train whistle sounded a second time. The chug and rumble of a powerful steam engine reached Josiah's ears. He swallowed down his despair. Help was too late!

As seconds passed, Crawford's face twisted wryly. Keeping his pistol pressed into Adam's side, he craned his thick neck and tried to peer through the trees.

"Where's that train?" he blurted worriedly. "It should've plunged into the ravine by now!"

Cursing, Crawford yanked Adam harshly and edged his way around the trees to the right and away from the bridge and ravine. With a nasty frown and with a tip of his head, he signaled Josiah to follow.

Josiah's legs twitched, ready to rush him far away from Crawford. But he knew if he tried, Crawford was mean enough to keep his threat and kill Adam.

Gripping his wet coat sleeve and fighting back tears, he forced himself to follow them.

Crawford gasped and stopped in the shadow of a leafy maple tree. The train, only a hundred feet away, was slowing. The engineer, his head and shoulders awash in dim yellow light, leaned out of the square side window and studied the moonlit tracks. In less than a minute, the engine would clear the stand of trees blocking the engineer's view of the bridge.

As Josiah crept close behind Adam, he saw Adam's lips begin to move. Through the sounds of rustling leaves and the night croakings of young frogs on the riverbanks, Josiah paused and listened as Adam started to whisper the Lord's Prayer.

Crawford tensed and glanced at Adam. With a snarl, Crawford cracked him on the side of the head with his pistol. Adam collapsed into the undergrowth near the edge of the trees.

Josiah wanted to reach down to help his friend but then pulled back. Someone had to be left standing to at least try to stop Crawford.

The vile, despicable words now spewing out of the Klansman's mouth hurt Josiah just as much as the wound in his arm. And the look in Crawford's bulging eyes was the most hateful he had ever seen. In that moment, Josiah guessed what Crawford was planning to do—he was going to board the train and run it into the river!

As if on cue, Crawford stalked across the grass toward the train.

His arm throbbing, Josiah stumbled after Crawford toward the slowly moving engine. Homes and a church had been burnt to the ground. Reverend Thompson had nearly died. Adam's father and his two henchmen had been shot dead before his eyes.

Josiah's legs wobbled, then stopped, as all of his remaining strength suddenly drained out of him. Thirty-three years earlier, Daniel Sweetwater hadn't been able to stop Crawford.

What could he really do to stop Crawford now? What could anybody do?

Even as Josiah's heart felt as if it would burst, his eyes were drawn upward to the heavens like the tip of a pin to a magnet. The stars seemed overly bright. Glistening. Alive. Watching.

Then Josiah knew. God wanted him to tell Jake Crawford the truth! The same truth that he had himself so painfully learned.

"Stop!" Josiah called out in a wavering voice just loudly enough for the Klansman to hear. "You can still turn back! Don't you know what God says? He's going to bring every work into judgment, every secret thing!"

Crawford paused and looked back. His right arm twitched. "Shut up, you little cur!"

"Daniel Sweetwater couldn't stop you. I can't stop you," Josiah said trembling, "but God can. He remembers Ellijay."

"Ellijay?" Crawford grunted as his eyebrows arched into sharp points. His mouth twisted cruelly. "When I heard your name a week ago in Vestry's office, I couldn't believe my luck. Found my little slave after all this time! Now I'm glad I didn't shoot you in that barnyard ten years ago. After you watch your colored-lovin' friends die, I'll get my trusty rifle and finish the job!"

The former plantation owner's words struck Josiah like a hammer. Once again the scene flashed before him: a rifle barrel jammed against his forehead, the silhouette of a large man looming over him, the roar and crackle of flames consuming the hay-filled barn and his parents. It hadn't been a bounty hunter that night, but Crawford himself who had come and hunted them down!

Crawford barked bitterly. "You do remember that night, don't you, boy?"

Then abruptly, his voice quieted and trailed off. "Yes, I'm sure you do."

He turned and stalked on through knee-high grass toward the crawling train.

The engineer pulled tighter on the brake lever and his eyes scanned the tracks. Steam spurted from the smokestack in thick, gray-white gusts. He did not see Crawford coming.

Through a blurry haze, Josiah struggled forward, his knees knocking together. By the time the engineer finally saw Crawford, the Klansman was only two steps away from the engine's compartment door.

Clutching his arm, Josiah stopped ten paces behind.

The locomotive rumbled to a halt. Crawford jerked open the metal door with one hand, his pistol in the other. Suddenly, bright yellow lantern light spilled from the engine room, momentarily stunning him.

The Klansman paused, his pistol not fully raised.

Josiah took another faltering step forward.

Standing inside the engine room were three men. A U.S. marshal stood with a shotgun aimed at Crawford's chest. The engineer had pressed himself back into the farthest corner from the door. Standing beside the marshal was a tall, straight-shouldered man with coarse black hair and a square jaw.

Josiah squinted. It was Daniel Sweetwater!

The U.S. Marshal edged his shotgun up until Crawford was staring down its double barrels.

"Don't even blink an eye," the marshal warned.

Movement from the right made Josiah glance in that direction. Two more marshals with shotguns stepped cautiously down the metal steps of the first passenger car thirty feet back. Josiah could see dozens of faces pressed up against the windows. Were Sam and Angelina watching?

The Delaware spoke, his voice deep and clear. "I always knew we'd meet again, Jake."

Crawford's hand tightened on his pistol. Josiah knew that only one bullet remained in the chamber.

"Meet again?" Crawford muttered. "Who in Hades are you?"

Daniel's face saddened noticeably. "Thirty-three years ago. Ellijay. The Cherokee Trail of Tears."

Crawford's mouth hung open. He cocked his head to one side and blinked. "Sweetwater?"

Crawford shifted his pistol in his hand. Josiah watched the southerner's forefinger slide against the trigger.

The Delaware continued with resignation in his voice. "Jake, those who live by violence, die by violence."

Josiah stepped sideways to see Daniel's face. To his surprise, Josiah saw no anger, no resentment, no hatred. All he could see was sorrow.

"Violence?" Crawford barked from between clenched teeth. "I'll show you violence!"

Crawford raised his pistol.

An explosion of white light split the darkness. Josiah turned his head as a deafening roar pounded in his ears. He looked up. He lifted his gaze to the engine compartment and avoided looking at Crawford's sprawled body in the grass.

Josiah's eyes met Daniel's. He saw no joy, only sadness.

Jake Crawford's time had come.

In this life and the next.

25

As Tuesday's festivities for the ten-year celebration of the Emancipation Proclamation moved toward starting time, Angelina MacDonald leaned over the bed and loosened the bandage around Josiah's left arm.

"Thanks," he replied. "That's a lot better."

Angelina noticed Daniel's book on the nightstand by his bed. "So, you've had some time to read."

Josiah nodded. "I've started writing some, too."

He paused for a moment before continuing. "With the Cherokee being treated so unfairly, Daniel's had to do a lot of forgiving over the years, hasn't he?"

"And he still does. Just like Toby and I still do—just like you will. Forgiving is never easy. And just forgiving, or being forgiven, doesn't fix every problem. But it's a starting place."

Returning to her chair by the desk, Angelina sat down and folded her hands in her lap. "Have you had a chance to see Adam?"

Josiah shook his head. "No, but Toby told me he's doing okay—as okay as he can be after watching his father murdered right in front of him."

Angelina sighed. "Comfort will be hard for him to come by. Public opinion of his father and his dark plans will cloud Adam's future. People will shun him. You know what injustice is all about. But you can relate to what he's gone through—is going through. What you both need is a fresh start."

Josiah met her thoughtful gaze. She was probably right. Adam had lost not only his job with the *Public Ledger,* but now he was without parents too. He and Adam shared something terrible, something so sad, it would stay with them all their lives. No matter what other people thought, Adam was a real hero. And a real friend.

A knock on the door caused them both to turn their heads. The door opened and Toby stuck his head in and looked at Josiah.

"You up to seeing visitors?"

Josiah nodded.

Toby pushed the door all the way open and then stepped to the side.

Sam MacDonald, the owner of the Freedom Press, entered the room. He was a few inches shorter than Toby and wore a brown suit and matching silk vest. His silver hair was brushed neatly back; his moustache was trimmed. He walked to the head of the bed and knelt down on one knee. He was not a physically imposing man, but his blue eyes sparkled with purpose and strength as he smiled at Josiah with admiration.

"You and Adam are brave and resourceful young men. When the engineer spotted Angelina's horse wandering up the tracks, he suspected there might be trouble ahead. And Toby told me what you said to Crawford there by the train—that held him up just long enough for the marshal and Daniel to position themselves in the engine compartment."

Josiah breathed deeply as he remembered Crawford's cruel eyes. "I just told him what God wanted him to hear, sir. Nothing more. But about Angelina's horse—I still can't figure out why she would stay by the tracks."

"God has his ways!" Toby exclaimed as he nodded his head to the right.

Josiah followed the motion of Toby's head.

Daniel Sweetwater stood silently in the doorway. Crow's feet sprang from the corners of his dark eyes, but otherwise, his smooth bronze face belied his age. Even having read his book, it was still hard for Josiah to believe that Daniel was fifty years old!

"Indeed, God has his ways," the Delaware said softly. "Jake

never understood that. All of his days he chose to serve his hatred. In the end, he could only choose destruction."

For several seconds, the room was silent.

Sam pushed himself to his feet and cleared his throat. "In the midst of tragedy, there's some good news. The mayor is meeting with various civic leaders as we speak to lower the tensions that have wracked this city. He's also setting up a committee to investigate Crawford's and Vestry's crimes.

"But of more personal and immediate importance," Sam continued, "is a proposition that Daniel would like to make to a young man who needs a new start, a young man who needs an opportunity to prove himself without someone second-guessing him."

Josiah's gaze was momentarily drawn to Toby's smiling face. The print shop manager winked.

Daniel folded his hands in front of him. "Next month, Sam and I are going back to Shawnee Mission, Kansas. He has agreed to help my son start a newspaper. Our paper will serve dispossessed Indian nations all across the Midwest. Toby tells me that you are one of the quickest apprentices east of the Mississippi. We could sure use your help in Kansas. We have a long way to go in the war for people's hearts and minds. Perhaps in time, you'll be running the paper with my son."

Sam nodded and grinned broadly.

Angelina leaned forward, elbows on her knees, her eyes beaming with excitement and approval. "You know, Josiah, when it counted, you chose the right side—God's side."

Shifting his position in the bed, Josiah turned and looked up at Daniel Sweetwater's face. Daniel extended his right hand. Their eyes met, and, for a moment, Josiah was sure he stared straight into Daniel's soul.

Josiah saw pools of great pain shadowed by a long, familiar sadness. Then, looking deeper, he saw flashes of joy, and hope, leaping like bright flames—a heart that would never stop fighting for freedom!

Josiah clasped Daniel's hand and smiled.

John and Mark live in Manassas, Virginia. In addition to writing The Century War Chronicles Freedom and Discovery Series, they are the co-authors of *Bloodlines*, a novel rich with historical detail, for high school readers and adults. From pre-Civil War America to the modern day, this fast-paced and thrilling story follows the lives of the MacDonald family who are called to contend with unseen powers of evil drawing bloodlines through history. Offering fresh insight into our nation's spiritual conflicts, past and present, *Bloodlines* inspires its readers to overcome life's deepest disappointments and to find faith in God.

Additional Reading

The KKK

Chalmers, David M. *Hooded Americanism: The First Century of the Ku Klux Klan 1865-1965*. Garden City, New York: Doubleday and Company, Inc. 1965.

Frost, Stanley. *The Challenge of the Klan*. New York: Negro Universities Press. 1969.

Grob, Gerald N., Editor. *Papers Read at the Meeting of Grand Dragons Knights of the Ku Klux Klan*. New York: Arno Press. 1977.

Tourgee, Albion Winegar. *The Invisible Empire*. Baton Rouge: Louisiana State University Press. 1989.

MacLean, Nancy. *Behind the Mask of Chivalry: The Making of the Second Ku Klux Klan*. New York: Oxford University Press. 1994.

Lay, Shawn. *Hooded Knights on the Niagara: The Ku Klux Klan in Buffalo, New York*. New York: New York University Press. 1995.

The Printing and Publishing Industry

McCorison, Marcus A. Editor. *The History of Printing in America*. New York: Weathervane Books. 1970.

Berthold, Arthur Benedict. *American Colonial Printing*. New York: Burt Franklin. 1970.

The Newspaper Industry

Waters, Sarah. *How Newspapers Are Made*. New York: Facts on File. 1989.

African American Issues

Henry, Christopher E. *Forever Free 1863-1875*. New York: Chelsea House. 1995.

Lowery, Charles D., Editor. *Encyclopedia of African American Civil Rights*. New York: Greenwood Press. 1992.

Berlin, Ira. *Freedom, A Documentary History of Emancipation 1861-1867*. Cambridge: Cambridge University Press. 1985.

Freedmen

In March of 1865, just prior to the end of the Civil War, the U.S. government created the Freedmen's Bureau. The Bureau's goal was to aid the newly freed slaves and help them become productive, self-supporting citizens. The Bureau created or helped create 3,695 schools, three universities and more than one hundred hospitals. The Bureau also distributed over twenty-one million food rations. The Bureau provided legal counsel, established a labor-management review board, and created an educational association.

Although many blacks remained in the South following the war, many fled northward. Without clear purpose or direction, often without food and ill-equipped to find work, former slaves often wandered homeless and destitute. Philadelphia, the city of brotherly love, the cradle of freedom, the home of the Declaration of Independence and the United States Constitution, became the destination of many former slaves, a group now collectively referred to as freedmen.

Even in the North, blacks were still often treated as second-class citizens, forced to ride in the backs of buses, and sit in separate facilities in restaurants. Though many whites worked tirelessly to change laws and open the minds of others to help promote equality, the problem of racism continued through ensuing decades and remains today one of the chief spiritual, social and political problems faced by Americans of all colors.

The Ku Klux Klan (KKK)

Immediately following the Civil War, the U.S. Government forced Reconstruction upon the Southern States. But Southerners, though no longer in control of their own state houses and city halls, remained strong in spirit. Indoctrinated for generations in the superiority of the white race, the average Southerner found it impossible to embrace former slaves as equals.

No longer able to control blacks by the whip and chain, many white Southerners now lived in fear. Most states of the former Confederacy refused to approve the Fourteenth Amendment to the Constitution, instead passing their own laws known as the Black Codes, or rules of conduct for former slaves, now called freedmen.

Tensions mounted. Race riots broke out in many major Southern cities. Small vigilante bands of white Southerners formed. Informally known as Regulators, these bands terrorized black communities, occasionally committing murder but always committing mayhem. The Regulators were the precursor to the deadly Ku Klux Klan.

The KKK emerged from southern shadows of hatred and fear sometime between December 1865, and May 1866, in the small town of Pulaski, Tennessee. The KKK began as a club, started by six former Confederate soldiers who were out of work and with time on their hands. Dressed in white sheets, wearing white hoods and riding similarly dressed horses, the club's initial purpose was simply the exercise of harmless pranks on the community. James Crowe, one of the six, stated emphatically that the original KKK was "purely social and for our amusement."

But soon the Klan's focus turned to intimidating former slaves. Club members began to frighten black men and women by claiming to be the ghosts of slain Confederate soldiers. Their escapades usually occurred after dark.

Club members named their group after the Greek word *kuklos* meaning "a circle." Modified to Ku Klux, the word Klan was added because of the Scottish-Irish heritage of the club's founders. Odd but meaningless occult symbols were soon added to the garb to provide a bizarre and curious appearance to the night predators.

It was not long until word spread concerning the club. Soon men from nearby communities had formed their own clubs or dens. And many of these dens simply imitated the official Klan's activities. Distinction between the true Klan and Klan impersonators became blurred.

At times, the Klan became so powerful in certain places that sheriffs, judges, respected business leaders and even ministers donned the white robes and hoods and terrorized the blacks in their communities. The Klan often ruled entire counties, exercising power and influence, and writing their own unofficial laws. The Klan was often called the invisible empire because it controlled entire communities from behind the veil of white hoods and robes.

The fear and hatred of blacks by many Southerners arose from a complex tangle of motivations and became the seedbed for the KKK's rise to influence. When slavery had been legal in the South, white slave holders often took advantage of their black female slaves. But once the slaves were emancipated and the Civil War ended, some white men feared that black men would retaliate against white women in revenge. Thus, any type of gesture, even friendly, of a black man toward a white woman could be interpreted as a prelude to rape.

Klan activities include lynching, the practice of stealing into the home of a black man who had glanced, smiled or tipped his hat to a white woman, rousting him from his bed, dragging him to a nearby tree, tying a rope around his neck, and hoisting him in the air until he strangled. Such atrocities often occurred in full view of his wife and children. Other KKK atrocities included tying up their captives, dousing them with gasoline or kerosene and burning them alive. Sometimes the ropes used for hanging were cut into pieces and sold as souvenirs.

Over the last 130 years, the trademark of the Klan is the flaming cross, placed upon the lawn of a black church or an outspoken proponent of civil rights. The burning cross has come to symbolize the power of the Klan to instill fear in the heart of the black community and those who support civil rights.

The Klan's primary sphere of influence remained in the Deep South, although the Klan reached its peak of influence in the 1920's, oddly enough in the state of Indiana. The Indiana Klan boasted 350,000 members, fully one tenth of the state's population at that time. The Klan's meteoric rise had an equally meteoric fall when its leader, D.C. Stephenson, was found guilty in a court of law of murdering a white woman, Madge Oberholtzer.

Even today, the KKK continues to exert influence. While Civil Rights reforms and legislation have limited many of the KKK's most heinous and overt activities toward blacks and other minorities, our current trend to stretch the boundaries of censorship and free speech has allowed the KKK to take a more active public stand. A simple search on the World Wide Web will yield dozens of links to KKK websites.

Racism and bigotry are problems of the human heart. One of the steps toward recognizing and ending racism is education. Even secular historians understand the value of knowing history. As philosopher George Santayana said, "Those who cannot remember the past are condemned to repeat it."